"What!" Meri answered in a squeaky tone.

"I just don't think I can get my slacks off over my bandaged foot."

She sighed. "Well, go ahead and take your pants off as far as you can. You *can* unbuckle your own belt and unzip your pants, can't you? If you just ease the pants down past your hips, I'll do the rest."

"Should we dim the lights or play soft music or something?" he asked, his mouth twitching into a smile.

She glared back. "If you want my help, you'd better cooperate."

"Oh, all right." Chet did the best he could, then motioned for Meri to take over. Her cheeks burned as she grabbed the slacks and tugged them toward his knees. It was all she could do to keep her eyes off his muscular thighs. It would have gone a lot faster if her hands hadn't been trembling so badly.

"Meri?"

"What now?"

"Could you help me under the covers?" Chet asked softly.

Meri pulled back the sheets and covered him as he lay down in the bed. She squelched a sudden urge to touch the soft dark hair on his chest.

"Meri?"

"What now?" she muttered, as embarrassed as she'd ever been.

"This." Before she could protest, he pulled her into his lap and took her breath away with a kiss that said more than good night. . . .

WHAT ARE *LOVESWEPT* ROMANCES?

They are stories of true romance and touching emotion. We believe those two very important ingredients are constants in our highly sensual and very believable stories in the *LOVESWEPT* line. Our goal is to give you, the reader, stories of consistently high quality that may sometimes make you laugh, sometimes make you cry, but are always fresh and creative and contain many delightful surprises within their pages.

Most romance fans read an enormous number of books. Those they truly love, they keep. Others may be traded with friends and soon forgotten. We hope that each *LOVESWEPT* romance will be a treasure—a "keeper." We will always try to publish

LOVE STORIES YOU'LL NEVER FORGET
BY AUTHORS YOU'LL ALWAYS REMEMBER

The Editors

NN

LOVESWEPT® • 159

Charlotte Hughes
Too Many Husbands

BANTAM BOOKS
TORONTO • NEW YORK • LONDON • SYDNEY • AUCKLAND

TOO MANY HUSBANDS

A Bantam Book / October 1986

Cover art by Barnett Plotkin.

LOVESWEPT® *and the wave device are registered
trademarks of Bantam Books, Inc. Registered in U.S. Patent
and Trademark Office and elsewhere.*

*All rights reserved.
Copyright © 1986 by Charlotte Hughes.
Cover art copyright © 1986 by Bantam Books, Inc.
This book may not be reproduced in whole or in part, by
mimeograph or any other means, without permission.
For information address: Bantam Books, Inc.*

*If you would be interested in receiving protective vinyl
covers for your Loveswept books, please write to this address
for information:*

> *Loveswept
> Bantam Books
> P.O. Box 985
> Hicksville, NY 11802*

ISBN 0-553-21792-5

Published simultaneously in the United States and Canada

PRINTED IN THE UNITED STATES OF AMERICA

O   0 9 8 7 6 5 4 3 2 1

To Kenny, my husband.

One

"You did what?" Meri Kincaid asked her daughter hotly, surprising them both and rendering the girl speechless for a moment.

Sixteen-year-old Bette stared back anxiously. "I—I said, I dropped Mr. Hanson's dog off for you," she repeated. "He called from the airport . . . said he'd just gotten in. He asked me to pick up Gretchen at the kennel."

"But *where* did you drop the dog off? What address?" Meri snapped her fingers vigorously as she talked, hoping to hurry the girl's answer.

"Woodbridge Apartments."

"Oh, no!"

"Mom, what did I do wrong?" Bette asked, her face a mask of confusion.

Without wasting another second, Meri plucked her worn clutch bag from the chair and shoveled through it for her car keys. Scraps of paper flew to the floor. "Honey, Tom Hanson doesn't live at Woodbridge," she said, crouching down to gather up the notes, lists, and other reminders she'd written to herself that had fallen from her bag. If she lost those, she might as well close down her business for good, she told herself. Never mind that half of the notes were outdated. She just hadn't had time to clean out her cluttered purse. "Mr. Hanson lives at Ridge Brook," she continued, rising from her kneeling position.

"Then who the heck lives at Woodbridge?"

"Bob Clay."

"Then, I—"

"You dropped the dog off at the wrong apartment." Meri snapped her bag closed and rushed to the front door.

Bette groaned and plopped down into an over-stuffed chair. "Oh, Mom—you know I can't keep up with all those men. Jeez!" She swung her legs over one worn arm and watched her mother's fruitless attempts to open the front door.

Meri tugged and twisted the knob on the ancient wooden door, the very same door that had been stuck when they'd moved into the house five years before. She wished to high heaven she could kick a hole through it. "It'll be okay, hon," she assured her daughter, hoping she was right in her assumption. "Why don't you try to call Bob for me and explain the mix-up?"

"Think he'll be mad?"

"Who knows?" Meri gritted her teeth and jerked hard. The door popped open, and she reeled backward. "Don't forget to call," she said as she regained her balance. She pulled the door closed and spun around.

She slammed right smack into her mother-in-law.

Paper sacks and purses overturned and hit the ground, combs and lipsticks and pens tumbling to the walk.

Plump arms akimbo, Aggie Kincaid glared at her daughter-in-law, her face red and splotchy from the late July heat. "Where's the fire?" she demanded in her sandpapery voice.

"Sooo sorry!" Meri cried, diving for the strewn items. She snatched up a plumber's helper. "What's this for?"

"Aw, the stupid plumbing is backed up again," Aggie grumbled, taking it from her. "Didn't you notice?"

"Haven't had time."

"I couldn't find the old plunger, so I had to go out and buy a brand new one." She clutched the wooden handle in one meaty hand and examined it. "D'you know how much they're charging for plungers these days?"

"No time to talk, Aggie," Meri interrupted, handing over the refilled sack and purse. "We've got problems." She backed down the walk, her own purse tucked under one arm. "Bette delivered Tom Hanson's dachshund to Bob Clay's apartment by mistake."

"Oh, no—"

"I've got to get over there right away. I'll work on the plumbing when I get back." One crisis at a time, please, she thought, getting into her Datsun. She nodded her good-bye, jerked the gear into reverse, and accelerated, shooting backward into the street. She froze as a car screeched to a halt behind her, blasting its horn. Quickly she rolled down her window and leaned out, hoping to make peace with the driver. Aggie beat her to it.

"Crazy fool!" she yelled, struggling with her bag. "You need to have your eyes examined, you know that?"

The man in the car leaned on his horn once more. Undaunted, Aggie stalked toward him, shaking the plunger at him as though it were a lethal weapon.

"How would you like to wear this around your neck,

mister?" she asked in her most strident, threatening tone.

Forgotten for the moment, Meri gunned her engine, wanting to flee the scene as quickly as possible—before blood was spilled, she thought wryly. She rolled her window up and flipped the air conditioner on high as she sped down the narrow street, running a stop sign. "That woman is going to have heart failure one of these days," she muttered, aiming the air vents at her face. She loosened the red scarf around her throat, silently cursing the Kansas City heat. No wonder everybody was in a bad mood, she thought. It had been weeks since the last rain and the temperature had continued to soar. But glancing out her window at the cloudless azure sky, she knew it would be even longer before they received the desperately needed rain, before the amber-colored lawns would have their thirst quenched. As well as everybody's temper.

Swerving quickly to her side of the road, Meri barely missed sideswiping a garbage truck. She hadn't driven more than a few more miles before her memory was jolted and flashed her the warning: interview with Mr. Ambrose! She groaned, gripping the steering wheel in frustration until her knuckles turned white. She glanced at her wristwatch. Six o'clock. Her appointment was for six-thirty. If she hurried, she could make it back home by six forty-five. Poor Mr. Ambrose. She had canceled on him twice already.

With one slender hand she lifted her honey-colored hair off the nape of her neck, which was damp with perspiration. Nothing had gone right all day, so why should she expect things to change now, for goodness' sake? Ever since she'd started this business of taking care of men, her own life had turned topsy-turvy. Now, five years later, it wasn't getting better; it was getting worse! There just weren't enough hours in the day to get everything done. All that cooking and cleaning and laundry and shopping— She rolled her eyes heavenward. Was there no end to it? Even with the additional help she'd hired, she and Aggie didn't have five minutes to spare these days.

Meri braked for a red light and shook her head in wonder. Who would have thought she and Aggie could pull it off, though, this business of caring for men? She sighed, thinking back to the days following Martin's death, when after twelve years of marriage she'd been forced to find a way to support herself and her daughter. Even with the insurance money fo fall back on, she'd been scared to death. Terrified.

Aggie had arrived for her son's funeral and offered to stay with Meri until she figured out what she was going to do. Meri had turned down her own parents' offer to move back home with them. At thirty the last thing she had wanted to do was go dragging back to her hometown of Polk City, Iowa, and live off her parents' generosity. She'd have to find a job. Stand on her own two feet for a change.

"I just don't know how to do anything," she had complained to Aggie one night when Martin had been dead less than a month. Oddly enough, she had grieved more for herself in those days than for her late husband.

Aggie had seemed to be only half-listening from her chair in front of the television set, watching a taped interview of several players from the Kansas City Royals' baseball team. "Nonsense," she had answered in a matter-of-fact tone. "You can do anything you want."

Meri's eyes brimmed with tears. "Sure," she said grimly, giving way to self-pity. "All I've done for the past twelve years is cook and clean." Why *had* she gotten married so young? she wondered for the umpteenth time. One fat tear rolled down her cheek.

"Nothing wrong with that," her mother-in-law answered, her eyes still glued to the set.

Meri sniffled and wiped her nose with a tissue. "Yeah, well, I don't see any ads in the newspaper for a wife," she said, irritated that Aggie seemed more interested in the evening news than with her problems.

"Hush!" Aggie ordered. "Did you hear what that man said?"

Meri blinked. "What man?"

"That one." Aggie pointed to a young male face on the TV screen. "He's a pitcher for the baseball team here and he's complaining about how bad single life is. So is his friend there." She pointed to the man beside him.

"What's that got to do with anything?"

"Don't you see?" Aggie said excitedly. "They need a wife!" She glanced around the room. "Where's the telephone book?"

"In the kitchen. What are you going to do?"

Aggie jumped from her chair and hurried toward the kitchen. "I'm going to call that pitcher . . . Tom Dixon . . . and tell him I've got a wife for him." Aggie located the telephone book on a countertop and began scanning the listings.

Meri was right behind her. "Are you crazy?"

"This could solve your problems."

"You've lost your mind, Aggie! I can't marry a complete stranger. I wouldn't even consider it."

"You don't have to marry the man," Aggie said. "All you have to do is take care of him the way a wife would."

"Oh, Aggie!" Meri's hand flew to her mouth. "You don't expect me to . . . to—"

"No, I don't expect you to sleep with the man, for Pete's sake!" Aggie growled impatiently. "Just take care of him. Haven't you ever heard of those women who have babies for other women?"

Meri frowned. "You mean . . . a surrogate mother?"

"Right. You could be a surrogate wife." Aggie

sounded pleased with her idea. "You could take care of several men as a matter of fact."

"Take care of them? In what way?" she asked suspiciously. Her voice had reached an odd pitch.

"You know, do the housekeeping, cooking, and laundry."

"It'll never work."

Aggie began dialing. "Just let me call this . . . what's his name, this Tom Dixon, and see what he thinks about the idea."

"I'm telling you, Aggie. It'll never work."

But it *had* worked. Not only for Tom Dixon, pitcher for the Kansas City Royals, but for several other men as well. All of the men had come to Meri by referral, and although she'd lost a couple of them to marriage, she had gotten many new referrals. Now she'd built up to a clientele of twelve men, and she and Aggie had become partners in a successful venture known as Wife, Inc.

"Twelve husbands," Meri said aloud, still finding it hard to believe after all this time. Who would have thought it would work? Better yet, who would have thought little ol' Merideth Anne Kincaid from Polk City, Iowa, would become a successful businesswoman by the time she was thirty-five years old? She grinned. And wouldn't Martin have flipped, knowing she'd done it all without him telling her how?

Turning into Bob Clay's apartment complex, Meri was reminded of the problem at hand and lost some of her zeal. Although it normally took twenty minutes to reach Bob's apartment, she'd made it in fifteen, despite the late afternoon traffic. A thought occurred to her. Perhaps Bob hadn't arrived home from work yet. If she were lucky, she could just grab the dog and run. Before Bob found out.

Meri wasn't so lucky. As she parked in front of Bob's building, she spotted his black Lincoln Continental. Sighing, she checked her reflection in the rearview mirror. It wasn't good. Expressive green eyes stared back at her and revealed her fatigue. Her collar-length pageboy drooped at the ends, and the side bangs fell in her eyes each time she moved her head. Her face was flushed and damp and her lips were without color. She quickly dug through her purse for her lipstick and swiped it across her mouth in one practiced motion. She blotted the excess with a used tissue, then tested her smile in the mirror, mentally rehearsing the apology she was about to make. She tried her best to smooth out the wrinkles in her red-and-navy print dress as she hurried across the parking lot to Bob's apartment. She came to a halt outside his door and knocked.

"I can explain everything," she chirped good-naturedly as Bob stuck his head through the crack in the door. A nervous bark sounded in the background.

"Gee, I hope so," he answered, stroking his red mustache. "Somebody's mutt just went to the bathroom on my white carpet."

Meri felt limp and drained by the time she arrived home more than an hour later after dropping Gretchen off to her thankful owner. The dog had barked nonstop during her ride as she raced back and forth across Meri's backseat. As a result, Meri's head had begun to throb, her blond hair was plastered to her skull, and her dress was now as wilted as a day-old corsage.

Although Bob Clay had been understanding about the mix-up with the dog, Meri had been thoroughly embarrassed. She'd used half a roll of paper towels on the carpet, and luckily the stain had come clean. Nevertheless, she'd promised to have the carpet professionally cleaned at her expense on the following day.

Meri frowned at the silver BMW that was parked in front of her house, reminding her once more of her appointment with Mr. Ambrose—her *late* appointment, she corrected herself, glancing at her wristwatch. She pressed her lips together, annoyed with the situation. Here it was, Friday, the end of a long and tiring week, and she hadn't had a bite to eat since breakfast. She was hot and tired and thirsty and her hands smelled like— She shuddered at the thought.

She parked her car and plodded up the oil-stained driveway. She should never have agreed to meet with the man in the first place. It had been all Aggie's doing because she liked the way he'd sounded over the phone. Just the thought of it irritated Meri even more. With twelve clients already demanding every minute, she certainly didn't have time for another. And the house was literally falling apart before her eyes. This fact was obvious once more as she tried to open the front door. "Darn door," she muttered crossly. She didn't have time for another client. She'd tell Mr. Ambrose to get lost!

Meri barely had time to get inside before Bette bounded down the stairs. "Guess what?" she asked, clearly excited, her blond curls dancing on her shoulders as she spoke. "Mr. Ambrose is here and he's helping Grandma unstop the commode."

"Oh, for heaven's sake." Meri pushed the door closed and slumped against it.

"Yeah, and Grandma's cussin' like you wouldn't believe. She's been telling him jokes."

"Which bathroom?"

"Upstairs."

Meri glanced in the direction of the stairs and shook her head, too exhausted for the moment to care. She waved the matter off and sunk into the nearest chair, dropping her purse to the floor. "Tell me this is all just a bad dream," she said, and moaned.

Bette knelt beside her and pulled off her high-heeled sandals. She massaged first one foot, then the other. "Poor Mom," she said soothingly, resting her head against her mother's knee. "It'll be okay."

"Ooooh, don't stop," Meri pleaded. "I knew there was a reason I kept you around, kid." She leaned back in the chair and closed her eyes, relaxing for the first time in days. This was just what she needed after running around like a crazy lady all week. Her taut muscles loosened and some of the tension in the back of her neck began to fade. Then her eyes shot open in horror. "Has Aggie told Mr. Ambrose the joke about the sailor?" she whispered.

Bette raised her head and grinned. "Uh-huh."

"Oh, no!" Meri jumped up from the chair, not a muscle in her body relaxed any longer. "I'd better get up there before Mr. Ambrose dies of embarrassment," she said. She slipped her shoes back on and raced toward the stairs.

Meri vaulted up the oak-paneled staircase two steps at a time, and heard laughter from down the hall. She winced. Another one of Aggie's bawdy jokes, no doubt. She paused just outside the bathroom door and tried to catch her breath and bring some kind of order to her appearance. Perhaps she could still bring it off, convince Mr. Ambrose they weren't all lunatics.

"Excuse me," she sang out, tapping lightly on the bathroom door. "May I come in?" She was answered with a chuckle from the other side, a sensual, throaty sound. She arched one brow. Whoever Mr. Ambrose was, he sure had one heck of a sexy laugh.

She stepped into the bathroom, took one look at Mr. Ambrose, and realized he was nothing like what she had expected. They stared at each other. From the expression on his face, which seemed to be one of outright shock, Meri gathered that Mr. Ambrose had stereotyped her as wrongly as she had him. He nodded once and one corner of his mouth lifted in a smile before he went back to work.

Although it was difficult to tell precisely his age,

Meri guessed him to be in his late thirties. He glanced
up intermittently as he worked, and the first thing
Meri was conscious of was his face—weathered and
tanned as though he literally lived in sunshine. He
continued to give her that peculiar half smile, half
smirk that suggested he found the situation amus-
ing. His nose was narrow and straight, running
between a pair of startling blue eyes. His head was
covered in a mop of salt and pepper curls that
matched exactly the bushy brows over each eye,
adding a rakish touch to his otherwise impeccable
appearance.

"I would shake hands with you, Mrs. Kincaid," he
finally said, looking up at her again, "but as you can
see—" He smiled and let the sentence drop as he took
the plunger from Aggie, who stood beside him, holding the various tools like a devoted surgical nurse.

Meri gazed down admiringly at his hands. They
were masculine but well kept, feathered with dark
hair that ran the length of each long, tapered finger.
They were strong hands, she noticed, that worked
effortlessly with the plunger, as though used to man-
ual labor. Yet they were gentle, too, and evoked a feeling of tenderness that surprised her. Hands for
caressing, she thought, mesmerized. His shirt-
sleeves were rolled up past his elbows, no doubt a pre-
caution taken to protect his starched white shirt. As
he worked the plunger against the opening of the toilet, he created sploshing and sucking noises that
made Meri wince.

Aggie continued to peer over the man's shoulders,
cursing the toilet for all it was worth. Before Meri
could say anything else, Mr. Ambrose flipped the
handle, giving the toilet a sound flushing. She covered her face with her hands.

"Well, I'll be damned!" Aggie exclaimed, shaking her
head. "You fixed it!" She slapped him on the back.

Meri dragged her hands slowly down the sides of

her face, aware that he was watching her, smiling at her. Actually he was grinning as though he'd break into hearty guffaws at the slightest provocation. His blue eyes scrutinized her, taking in her appearance, which she knew was nothing less than gauche at the moment. Nevertheless, she raised her head proudly, and mustering up every bit of self-confidence and poise she could find, held out her hand and introduced herself.

"Chet Ambrose," he said, returning the introduction.

"Pleased to meet you," she answered, giving him her best professional smile. The smile faded as her fingers closed around the slim wooden handle of the plunger.

"Why on earth did you get that man involved with our plumbing problem, Aggie?" Meri whispered once they were outside the bathroom, leaving Chet inside to wash up.

"He fixed it, didn't he?" Aggie said, shrugging as she led the way downstairs. "I told him if he fixed it, he could stay for dinner."

"Oh, Aggie, you didn't."

"Sure did. I made spaghetti sauce today." She glanced over her shoulder at her daughter-in-law. "About two gallons, as a matter of fact. I'll just warm some of it up." She hurried into the kitchen and Meri followed her like a lost puppy. "Why don't you pour Chet some wine?" Aggie suggested. "We still have that unopened bottle we bought last Christmas. I stuck it in the freezer about twenty minutes ago to chill. And hand me the lettuce out of the fridge."

Meri did as she was told, moving about in a daze. "Aggie, what's going on?" she finally asked, coming out of her stupor. "First you invite the man to dinner, then you want me to bring out the wine—" She clutched the head of lettuce tightly, determined to get some answers before passing it to her mother-in-law.

"Okay," Aggie said as though she couldn't care less. "But you're going to feel silly giving him tap water in a jelly glass when you find out who he is." She took the head of lettuce Meri handed her. "Yeah, I figured that would get your attention."

Meri edged closer. "Well? Who is he, for goodness' sake?"

"He's Handy-Andy," Aggie said smugly.

"Who?"

"Oh, you know who I mean. He owns all those fix-it stores. Paint and wallpaper and lumber. Stuff like that." She moved to the sink.

Meri was genuinely impressed. "You mean he owns those big Handy-Andy Hardware stores?" she whispered excitedly.

"Uh-huh." Aggie began tearing apart the lettuce leaves.

"And you let him go crawling around in our bathroom?" Meri asked, horrified. "That's just great! Next we'll have him dig up the septic tank." She stalked back to the refrigerator and jerked open the freezer door. "Well, I don't care who he is," she muttered. "We don't have time for another client. I don't know why I let you talk me into meeting with him in the first place, but—"

"All cleaned up," Chet announced from the doorway, effectively cutting off the rest of Meri's sentence. "I don't think you'll be having any more trouble with it," he continued, rolling his shirt-sleeves down over his wrists, "but if you do, let me know and I'll order some new parts." He smiled at Meri. "Better close that freezer door," he said lightly. "You're letting all the cold air out."

Meri blushed and quickly closed the door. She glanced in his direction once more and was instantly awarded another brilliant smile showing nice healthy-looking teeth. "Uh, would you like a glass of wine?" she asked hesitantly, overcome for a moment by his charm. She held up the bottle of pale honey-colored liquid. "It's not the best quality, but it's cold," she added, then wondered at her remark. Why was she making excuses about the wine?

"Are you going to have some?" he asked.

It was not an unreasonable question, but the effect his words had on her were the same as if he'd just asked, "Are you planning to sleep with me?" Meri felt her heart quicken and she almost choked on her reply. "Uh, yes, I was thinking of it," she finally managed.

"I do think you need a drink," Aggie mumbled.

Meri disregarded the remark. "Mr. Ambrose—"

"Call me Chet."

"Uh, Chet . . ." She swallowed. "Why don't you make yourself comfortable in the living room?" she suggested, trying to get him out of the kitchen so he wouldn't watch her every move. She was beginning to feel terribly self-conscious for some reason. "I'll bring a glass of wine out to you in just a second." He nodded and left, and she sighed with relief. She opened a drawer and began digging for a corkscrew. "Aggie, would you mind getting me the crystal wineglasses?" she asked, still searching for the corkscrew.

Aggie glanced up at her. "Crystal? I didn't know we had any."

"In the hutch in the dining room," Meri said, but seeing Aggie's blank look, added, "the ones we use at Christmas."

"Oh. Well, why didn't you say so?" Aggie dried her hands on her apron as she went. She returned a few minutes later carrying three long-stemmed wine-glasses. "What s'matter with you?" she asked, giving Meri a funny look. "You're as edgy as a coon in hunting season. And we don't ever use these glasses. And how come you're trying to find a corkscrew to open a three-dollar bottle of wine?"

Meri slammed the drawer closed and covered her eyes, wishing the night was over with. "It's that man," she whispered. "He's making me a nervous wreck." She took a deep breath and twisted the metal cap off the bottle. "Don't stand there gawking at me like I've just grown horns," she said to Aggie.

"Bothers you, does he?" Aggie asked, grinning.

"Mind your own business." Meri poured the wine and handed a glass to Aggie. "And wipe that grin off your face." She picked up the two remaining glasses and tried to ignore her mother-in-law's soft cackling as she left the room.

Chet looked completely at home in the worn, over-stuffed chair beside the fireplace. His khaki-colored jacket, which matched his snug-fitting slacks, was draped across the back of the sofa. He stood as soon as Meri entered the room and she tried not to notice how his white shirt hugged his broad chest. The two top buttons had been undone, laying the collar open, and a few sprigs of dark hair curled sensuously over the starched material. The shirt was almost lumi-nous in contrast to his deep tan. Meri offered him one of the wineglasses.

"I've been meaning to tell you how much I like your house," he said, taking the goblet from her. His fingers brushed hers briefly and caused her stomach to flutter as though it were made of butterfly wings. She glanced away quickly, embarrassed by her own response, but if he noticed, he gave no indication. "Do you think we could fit in a tour before dinner?" he asked.

She looked up in surprise, taken aback by his forward manner. She glanced around the room, reaffirming that they were alone. Aggie was busy preparing dinner and Bette was in the middle of one of her lengthy telephone conversations. That could only mean one thing: He expected her to give the tour.

"Unless you don't want to," he added, as though reading her thoughts.

"There's not much to see," she answered, trying to shift her gaze away from his intense eyes.

"I understand there are three floors."

"Four if you count the basement. The third floor is an apartment. That's where Aggie does all the cooking for our clients." Meri allowed herself to look again at his eyes and wondered how she could have torn her gaze away in the first place.

"Sounds nice."

"It needs a lot of work. Actually . . ." She paused and smiled. "The whole place needs a lot of work. That's why it was so . . . affordable." She frowned. Now she was making excuses about the house.

"I'd certainly like to see the rest of it," he said, raising his glass to his lips. He took a sip of wine, and she watched in fascination as his Adam's apple dipped when swallowing. His neck was not thick like some of the men she knew, some of her middle-aged clients, but was lean and corded with muscles.

"Are you interested in old houses?" she heard herself ask.

"You might say that. It's become a hobby with me lately."

He gave her another one of those smiles. Her pulse quickened. How could she say no to a smile like that? She couldn't. "Okay, follow me," she said, her own lips curling at the corners. "You've already seen most of the ground floor. I'll let you take a quick peek at the bedrooms if you promise not to look at the clutter." She was about to set her wineglass down, but decided to keep it instead. She needed to hold on to something, even something as insubstantial as a delicate crystal goblet. She led him toward the stairs, clutching the glass as though it offered some kind of protection.

She took the stairs slowly, glancing over her shoulder self-consciously as he followed close behind. Too close, she noticed, and picked up her pace. Once upstairs, she opened bedroom doors, allowing him to inspect each room. Did he seem unusually interested in her bedroom, or was it just her imagination? "You've already seen the . . . er . . . bathroom," she said, passing by the door.

"I wasn't really paying that much attention," he said, opening the door and going in. Meri backed up and waited just outside. "I like your sink and tub," he said, smiling with approval at the antique pedestal sink and clawfoot bathtub. "I've got something back at the store that would shine them up like new. I'll have to remember to bring it by."

Meri watched him as he continued to inspect the house. To her surprise, he seemed to have more than a casual interest in it. Several times he stopped to look at molding or pound the walls or inspect light fixtures. She smiled as she remembered how delighted she'd been when she first saw the house, before she had become overwhelmed with how much work it needed. It would probably take the rest of her life to fix it up.

"I'm glad someone else appreciates old things," she said once he'd finished inspecting an old wall lamp in the hall. It had never worked. One day she would hire an electrician to repair it. When there was time . . . and, of course, money. "Aggie hates this place," she went on, hoping he didn't notice where the molding was chipped and cracked or where the carpet was stained and threadbare. She was certain he did though. Those blue eyes didn't miss a thing.

"I think it's wonderful," he said, "I've never seen anything like it."

"Well, it *is* unusual," she agreed, heading for the

stairs. "I believe it was listed with the realtors as an antique-hunter's dream." She laughed softly. "Aggie calls it a nightmare."

He chuckled. "What made you decide to buy it?" he asked.

"You mean beside the fact it was cheap?" Another laugh. She was feeling more at ease with him. "We needed more room after Aggie moved in . . . especially with starting the business and all." She smiled shyly. "It's hard to find a house with two kitchens."

"May I see the apartment?" he asked, motioning to the stairs leading to the third floor.

"It's only three rooms."

He answered with a lazy half smile. "Indulge me."

That smile again, she thought, her heart hammering in her chest. She led him up the short flight of stairs and opened the door to the apartment, then stepped aside so he could enter the sparsely furnished living room. "It's hot up here this time of day," she said as he walked into the room. She followed him. "Aggie runs the air conditioner in the mornings while she does the cooking." She stopped short, unnerved that he chose to stand so close while she talked. "I'll show you the kitchen if you like," she offered, hurrying into the next room. She needed to put some distance between them.

Chet gave a low whistle as he entered the kitchen, which was the largest room in the apartment. Covering one wall were at least three dozen pots and pans in various shapes and sizes, many of them several times larger than those used for normal cooking. Shelves along another wall contained cafeteria-style trays, individual casserole dishes, metal pie pans, loaf pans, and various baking utensils. Stacked neatly to one side of the room were dozens of gallon-sized canned goods, containing green beans, corn, peas, peaches, and other sliced fruits.

"It looks like a restaurant," Chet said, shaking his

head at the conglomeration. "Who are you feeding? The Jolly Green Giant?"

Meri laughed. "It *should* look like a restaurant," she said, crossing her arms as she leaned against a cabinet. "We order most of this through a restaurant supply house. When you cook for a dozen men, it's like cooking for a small army."

He shook his head. "How did you ever get started in this business, Meri? If you don't mind my asking."

She realized it was the first time he'd said her name. She glanced down at the linoleum floor, shifting her feet nervously. "Of course not," she answered. There was no noise coming from downstairs. Complete silence. It gave her an odd feeling, as though they were cut off from the rest of the world. "I got started in this shortly after my husband died," she finally said, not allowing herself to meet the eyes she felt watching her.

"Was that very long ago?"

"Five years." She forced herself to look up. She couldn't very well stand there talking to the floor. "He . . . uh, Martin died in an automobile accident."

Chet nodded slowly, as though digesting each tidbit she tossed at him. "And is that how you and Aggie came to live together?"

Meri nodded absently, noticing the way the late afternoon sun sliced through the window and bathed his tanned face in light. His eyes were without a doubt the clearest shade of blue she'd ever seen, surrounded by thick, stubby lashes. On the outer edges of each eye a network of fine tiny creases darted out and disappeared into his graying temples. The effect was striking, she decided, if not overly handsome. He shifted slightly and she realized she was staring. She cleared her throat. "As you can see," she said, turning for the doorway, "there's a sitting room and bedroom as well." She heard his soft chuckle from behind and turned, surprised at the look he gave her.

"I don't mean to laugh," he said, walking toward her. "It's just that I'm amused—or bemused— because I've never met a twosome like you and Aggie before. You're complete opposites, you know. Aggie's so—" He paused as though trying to think of just the right word. "So straightforward." He shook his head and laughed again. "But you're different. Reserved. Are you that way with everybody or just with me?"

Meri was thankful she'd carried her wineglass with her, and hung on to it now as though her very life depended on it. "I don't know what you mean," she said, her gaze scanning the floor once more.

"Are you afraid of me, Meri?"

She looked at him, half expecting to see a smile on his face, but there was none. He looked thoughtful and sincere. He'd come closer, terribly close, so close he blocked the doorway leading to the next room. Not that she had any intention of darting out of the room or anything like that, she told herself. "Why should I be afraid of you?" she asked in a tone that suggested she found the idea ridiculous. "I hardly know you." She raised her glass to her lips and tasted the liquid, peering at him from over the rim. A drop of wine spilled onto her bottom lip and she slid her tongue across her lip to retrieve it. Chet watched.

"That's right," he finally said. "You don't know me, do you?" He set his wineglass down carefully on the counter and gave her a reckless smile. "Then I hope you won't hold it against me—"

She watched him move forward, noticed the way his head tilted slightly, but whatever she might have expected, she certainly didn't think he was going to kiss her! But he did. In one fluid motion he lowered his mouth over hers and captured her lips in a warm, delicious, wine-scented kiss. Her reaction, something akin to shock, caused her to sway, and she almost dropped her wineglass. Chet steadied her, placing a firm hand at the small of her back. Then that hand began a devilish caress along her spine as the kiss deepened into a mind-boggling experience. Meri didn't budge. She couldn't. Her brain had obviously disappeared or turned to mush, and by the time she located it and ordered it into action, Chet had raised his head and the kiss had ended as quickly as it had begun. Her eyes were wide with astonishment. She didn't know what to say. What *could* she say?

"I'm sorry," he whispered, his breath warm and sweet on her face. "I couldn't help it. I've wanted to kiss you since I first laid eyes on you. I guess we should go back downstairs now, huh?"

She nodded, her brain slowly coming back to life. Somehow she managed to find her way out of the apartment with Chet following close behind. She glanced back at him once and thought he didn't look the least bit contrite about his actions.

Two

By the time they had finished a hearty spaghetti dinner, Chet Ambrose had managed to captivate both Aggie and Bette. They listened as he shared anecdotes of his years with the Handy-Andy Hardware chain, entertaining them for more than two hours. While he talked, Meri watched him closely. He gave no indication they'd kissed in the upstairs apartment. But then, how were complete strangers supposed to act after they'd shared a kiss? She didn't have an answer for that. She'd never been one for casual necking, and if one of her clients had even *dared* such a thing, she would have given him a tongue-lashing he would never have forgotten. So why had she let Chet get away with it? And why the heck was she so uncomfortable around him? She was used to dealing with men on a daily basis. All kinds of men.

She shifted in her chair and silently chided herself for making such a big deal out of it. People kissed each other all the time and for almost no reason. Yes, but when it was over, they didn't stand there all tongue-tied and goggle-eyed like she had. It wasn't the kiss that bothered her so much, but the way she had reacted. She'd liked it. A lot. That's what *really* had her concerned. As a matter of fact, it scared the daylights out of her!

"I'd love to own a place like this," Chet said, breaking into Meri's thoughts.

"Make us an offer," Aggie said. She held her wineglass up for him to refill, ignoring Meri's look of warning.

Chet laughed, his blue eyes clearly revealing his amusement. "You would appreciate this place more, Aggie, if you'd just spent the last month in a hotel."

"Are you planning on moving to the area permanently?" Meri asked. For some reason, the idea was not altogether unpleasant. She supposed she could live with sweaty palms. Chet turned his attention back to her and his gaze swept appreciatively over her face. She didn't feel as self-conscious as she had earlier, before she'd freshened up. She'd also touched up her makeup and brushed her hair.

"Sooner or later," he answered. "I've already sold all my holdings in Texas and Oklahoma. I don't have any reason to go back."

"Do you plan to sell your stores here as well?"

He shrugged. "If somebody offers me the right price." He leaned forward on his elbows. "The hardware business doesn't hold much interest for me these days."

"What *does* hold your interest?" she asked in a crisp tone that was almost challenging. She regretted it instantly, having caught Bette's and Aggie's attention. For a second, although it seemed an eternity, all three merely stared at her.

"You'd probably laugh if I told you," he said, and his smile eased the sudden tension in the room. He picked up his wineglass, but his eyes remained fixed on Meri's, probing them as though he were trying to pick his way past them and find her thoughts. He twirled the glass, rolling the stem back and forth between this thumb and forefinger.

"Tell us anyway," Bette demanded enthusiastically. It was obvious Chet had won her over.

He continued twirling the glass, letting the wine slosh gently up one side and down the other. Then he set it down. "To tell you the truth, I'd much rather putter around an old house than involve myself with the stores. A house like this one, that is." He smiled again. "I've renovated a couple of houses in the past few years, nothing quite like this, of course." He glanced around the room. "This house would be a challenge."

"Don't let us stop you," Aggie said matter-of-factly. "We need all the help we can get."

He seemed to ponder the idea. "You know, this place would make a good promotional piece for my stores."

Meri rested one elbow on the table and propped her chin on her hand. "What do you mean?"

"The kinds of things advertisers do with dieters," he said, grinning. "Show people before and after pictures of what their house can look like if they shop at my stores. I could have brochures printed. Maybe it would boost sales and those sales might get me an interested buyer."

"You sound like you really want to sell," Meri said. "Why not sit back and enjoy your success?"

He was silent for a moment, then said, "I guess I'm not the big businessman I used to be. Too much work can burn a person out." He smiled. "I've sort of changed my way of thinking in the last year or so."

"Is that what prompted you to sell the other stories?" she asked. "This new way of thinking." She was being nosy and she knew it, but couldn't help herself.

Chet didn't seem to mind. "You might say I've . . . er . . . rearranged my priorities." His intent gaze seemed to tell her that he knew this bit of information was only an enticement.

Meri didn't press him. If she was any judge of character, she could guess that Chet Ambrose was the type of man who would disclose only as much information about himself as he was ready to. Not that she had any intention of interrogating him. Why should she give a hoot what he decided to do with his life?

"Yes, I can see all kinds of possibilities in this place," he said, changing the subject.

"He's not as bright as I thought he was," Aggie commented.

Chet accepted the remark good-naturedly. "Why, you ladies have a palace here and don't even realize it."

Aggie snorted. Bette giggled. Meri leaned forward and listened. "How do you figure that?" she asked.

"Just look at this place," he said, holding his arms out. All three women glanced around the room expectantly, trying to discover the source of his excitement. None of them looked impressed as they returned their attention to him. Nevertheless, Chet didn't lose any zeal over it. "The first thing I'd do is rip up every shred of carpet," he said in a professional voice.

"I realize we need new carpeting," Meri said, "but Aggie and I haven't had time to shop for it and I'm not sure we could afford to do the entire house."

"I wouldn't think of putting carpet down on these floors," he said as though the mere thought was sheer lunacy. "Do you have any idea what lies beneath all this carpet?"

"We try not to think about it," Meri answered dryly.

"Wood floors, ladies," he announced. "I'm willing to bet they're in good shape too. And that's not all." He pointed upward. "That molding up there. Have any idea how old that is?"

The women lifted their gazes to the intricately

carved wood that adorned the upper section of the wall. "I'm sure it's as old as the hills," Meri said, "but it's chipped and cracked—"

"And can be restored," he interrupted. "Everything in this house can be restored or repaired." He grinned. "Even the plumbing."

"Yeah, with a lot of money," Aggie said, taking a sip of wine. "Not even the government has that kind of money."

"All this sounds wonderful, Chet," Meri began in a contrary tone, "but Aggie and I can't really afford a major overhaul on this place."

"Y'know what we ought to do?" Aggie said, refilling her wineglass and offering more. When he declined, she placed the bottle next to her glass. "What we should do here," she continued, "is swap talents."

Meri winced, hearing the slur in her mother-in-law's voice, afraid she might be getting a bit tipsy. "Would anyone like coffee?" she asked quickly, hoping to put a halt to the conversation. She was suddenly unsure of which direction Aggie was trying to lead it.

"I'd like a cup," Chet said.

"None for me," Aggie said, once again ignoring the hard stare Meri gave her.

Meri stalked into the kitchen to start the coffee while trying to listen to the ongoing conversation in the next room. Unfortunately Bette picked that particular moment to start clearing off the table and her clatter cut off the voices from the other room. By the time Meri returned to the dining room balancing a tray of coffee cups, Chet and Aggie seemed to be pondering something between themselves.

"Did I miss anything?" Meri asked anxiously.

Chet glanced up at her, his expression dazed. When he saw the tray, he stood quickly, took it from her, and placed it on the table. Then he scratched his head in a way that told Meri he was either uncomfortable, confused, or undecided about something. "Aggie just made me a proposition," he finally said, reclaiming his seat.

"Oh?" Meri began to pass out the coffee cups, her gaze darting nervously to her mother-in-law. She placed a cup of coffee beside Aggie, hoping she would change her mind and drink it. Aggie looked like she was very pleased with herself at the moment. "Well?" Meri asked, glancing from one to the other. "Are you going to let me in on it?"

"Aggie has suggested we work a trade," Chet said, leaning back in his chair. He cocked his head to the side and studied her, waiting for her reaction. "I offer my services in exchange for yours."

Meri scooped a teaspoon of sugar into her coffee and stirred. "I don't understand."

"I make repairs on this place for you and you take care of my . . . er . . . domestic chores." He glanced down at his coffee cup, his face void of expression.

Aggie drained the contents of her wineglass and slammed it onto the table, causing both Meri and Chet to jump. "He could live here while he does the work," she announced loudly, as though she were broadcasting a blue-light special at K mart. "It would make it easier for us to take care of him."

Meri stared at her mother-in-law in disbelief. She was joking, of course. No, she could tell from the look on Aggie's face that she wasn't joking. "Live here?" she said, her irritation mounting. "And just *where* would you suggest he live?"

"On the third floor."

Meri shook her head, then smiled at the two conspirators as though she were indulging them both in some childish fantasy. "It all sounds wonderful," she said in a sugary tone, "but we need that space for cooking. That's one of the reasons we bought the house in the first place, remember?" She aimed the question directly at her mother-in-law.

"That wouldn't be a problem for me," Chet said. "Aggie could still use the kitchen."

"Because he would be taking all his meals with us," Aggie added. "You wouldn't have to deliver any more dinners than you already do."

Meri said nothing, not daring to look in Chet's direction. Bette had stopped rinsing dishes in the kitchen and was lurking in the doorway. The very air in the room seemed to be crackling, Meri thought.

"I hope you don't mind Aggie suggesting it," Chet said when Meri remained silent.

She glanced up at him. "No, of course not," she lied. How in the world would she be able to eat, sleep, and bathe in the same house with the man? "This house is as much Aggie's as it is mine," she added. "She has every right to make some of the decisions here." She paused for a moment, trying to choose her words carefully. "It's just . . . I'm afraid you might find it a bit . . . uncomfortable with three women living beneath you, all around you."

"On the contrary," he said, that delicious smile reappearing, "I think it would be delightful. But, of course, the decision rests with you."

Much to her discomfort, Meri found three sets of eyes focused on her. They waited, she knew, for her answer. It would be impossible with him living in the same house, she thought, and her instinct warned her to say no. Yet, she hated being the bad guy. And the work was desperately needed. If he stayed in the apartment . . . out of her way . . . "Have you any idea how long it will take to make the renovations?" she asked.

He shrugged. "A matter of months."

He wasn't even going to give her a firm date. "What's it going to cost us?" she asked, squirming in her chair.

He shook his head. "Not a cent. That's part of the deal. I'll do the work at my expense—or should I say at

Handy-Andy's expense.—provided you'll agree to let me take pictures of the entire process. For my brochure," he added, as if to remind her.

She sighed, watching Bette jump up and down excitedly in the doorway. The girl looked like she was about to pop. "Well—" She paused, knowing she was about to make a big mistake. "As long as you're going to turn this place into a circus, it might as well have three rings." She closed her eyes, feeling frustrated with the whole thing. "Okay," she finally agreed. "We can give it a try. If things don't work out—"

"I'll move immediately."

"And no hard feelings?"

"No hard feelings," he agreed easily. He looked at Aggie and winked, then raised his coffee cup in a toast. "See, I told you I could talk her into it," he whispered loud enough for everybody to hear.

Meri wasn't smiling. "I hope you won't be disappointed," she said, her tone cool. "We aren't offering as much in this deal as you are."

"Don't be so sure," he said. "A man likes to feel needed once in a while. And I think you probably need a husband just as badly I need a wife."

"Why would a man like that want to live in a place like this?" Meri pondered aloud as she and Aggie sipped their first cup of coffee of the morning in the breakfast nook adjacent to the kitchen. More than a week had passed since Chet had dined with them and discussed plans for moving in, and Meri had not yet chased him from her thoughts. She could still taste his kiss, remember how his lips had felt on hers, warm and firm and very nice. It was the last thing she thought about each night before she drifted off to sleep. He had contacted Aggie once to talk over his moving plans, which he'd postponed until the end of the month because of business, and Meri had assumed it was his way of backing out. She was almost thankful. Thankful, but disappointed.

She was wearing thin cotton pajamas, already beginning to cling to the damp areas of her body because of the heat. The ancient air conditioners, despite their constant sputtering, couldn't significantly lower the temperature. Lethargic after a long and hectic week, she hiked one leg up in her chair, propped her chin on her knee, and glanced around the breakfast nook. She despised the room. Never having had a flair for decorating, she had scanned *Better Homes & Gardens* for days after they'd first moved into the house. She'd been smitten by the bold colors used by some of the professional decorators and had chosen the colors red, white, and blue for this room. It looked awful. She knew it, Aggie knew it, and Bette knew it. But neither Aggie nor Bette knew she knew it and so they said nothing critical about the breakfast room, her first and last attempt at redecorating the century-old house. "I'll bet he can afford the nicest hotels in town," she said, thinking out loud. "So why would he want to move into a dingy three-room apartment?"

Aggie, whose mood was always darkest in the morning, muttered something about why a normal, healthy, red-blooded woman would not welcome a man like Chet Ambrose in her life.

"He's not my type," Meri answered.

Aggie looked at her long and hard from over the rim of her coffee cup. "What's that supposed to mean?"

"Just look at him," Meri said matter-of-factly. "He has all that money, plus the stores, and what does he want to do? He wants to sell out and putter around an old house. Talk about ambition! I'll bet he's never worked a day in his life. Probably inherited the stores from his father."

Aggie pulled her cotton robe over her ample bosom and grunted. "And how did you come about this vast knowledge of men, madam?" she asked. "When's the last time you went out with one?"

"You know the answer as well as I do," Meri said. "I don't have time to date." She stretched her long legs out before her and wiggled her toes, trying to shake off her laziness. "Anyway, I haven't met anyone who interests me."

She glanced at the wall clock and saw it was time to get going. She had a busy morning ahead of her. She drained her coffee cup. "If you're worried about Chet Ambrose," she said, "forget it. He's had time to reconsider and if he's half as smart as I think he is, he'll bow out. I doubt either of us will see him again."

Meri slipped into a pair of designer jeans and a white cotton blouse, going over in her mind once more what she had to do that morning. It was Saturday, her day for collecting schedules from her clients in preparation for the following week. It would take much of the morning to visit with them, then she would be free for the rest of the weekend. Free! Free to do what? she wondered, stepping into loafers. This was not a problem she encountered often. How would she spend her time? Bette was away for two weeks with a friend and her family, so that put an end to any aspirations Meri might have had about a mother-daughter weekend.

She was still trying to figure out how she would spend her afternoon when she came downstairs a few minutes later. She'd barely reached the landing when the front door bell pealed out. Steeling herself, she tugged forcefully at the doorknob and jerked the door open. A young man stood on the other side carrying camera equipment.

"Chet Ambrose sent me," he announced. "I'm supposed to take pictures."

"Of what?" she inquired, her eyes narrowing with suspicion.

He glanced down at the piece of paper in his hand.

"Peeling paint, cracked molding, sagging dry-wall . . ." He paused and looked up. "Did I come to the right place?"

Meri nodded, pursing her lips in irritation. The thought of a perfect stranger taking pictures of her house irked the daylights out of her. But she had already made a deal with Chet Ambrose, and like Aggie had been saying all week, a deal was a deal. She stepped aside to allow the photographer to enter. "Where's Mr. Ambrose?" she asked.

He shrugged. "I've never met the man. I was hired over the telephone to take pictures, that's all. Name's Bill." He set his camera bag and tripod on the floor. "I'm a free-lance man. I'm supposed to take pictures for some kind of brochure or catalog. Something like that. How old is this place anyway?" he asked, looking around.

"Prehistoric. Where do you want to start?"

Bill peered around the alcove into the living room, taking in the ceiling and walls. "I'll need to set up some lights," he muttered, as though talking to himself. "Is this about as bad as it gets?"

Meri glared at the back of his head. "No," she answered in a saccharine tone. "As a matter of fact, this is one of the nicer rooms."

"Hmmm. This is going to take longer than I thought. I'll probably need more film too."

An hour later he was still taking pictures. Meri was fuming in the kitchen. "Do you believe the nerve of that guy out there?" she asked Aggie. "He wanted to know who the drunk was that painted the breakfast room."

"At least he's honest. I should never have let you talk me into helping you buy this place."

"Here we go again."

"If you had any sense, you'd let Chet fix this place up so we could sell it."

"Sell it?" Meri wailed.

"That's right. Maybe we could make a few bucks and get rid of the biggest headache we've ever had."

"Then what?"

Aggie shrugged. "I don't know about you, but I'd probably buy me one of those retirement villas on the other side of town. I hear they have some wild Saturday-night poker games."

"But what about the business?" Meri asked, incredulous.

"You could hire a real cook for half of what you're paying me. Anyway, I'm getting too old for all this work."

Meri threw her hands up in frustration. "Great! I've got a cleaning lady who is too pregnant to clean, a daughter too lazy to help out, and a mother-in-law who claims she's too old to work. On top of that," she continued, her voice growing shrill, "I've got a complete stranger moving into my house and—" She looked closely at her mother-in-law. "And don't you *dare* think you're going to move into your villa while Chet Ambrose is living under this roof!" She had to stop to catch her breath. "And if all that weren't bad enough, I've got some maniac upstairs taking pictures of the rust stains in my bathtub and toilet bowl!"

"Well, don't worry about me," Aggie said as though she were about to be thrown to the lions. "If I'm going to die, I might as well die working. One day I'm going to keel over right here in front of this stove."

"Oh, Lord, Aggie," Meri said, wincing as though she were in pain. "Please don't talk like that. You know I'd die if something happened to you. Don't make things worse than they are." She pressed her fingers to her temples. Her head was beginning to throb. "Do you mind if we talk about this later?" she asked, giving her mother-in-law a quick peck on the cheek. "I've got to go!"

*   *   *

By the time Meri had taken care of most of her clients, she had a splitting headache. Although each man had seemed pleased with the service he was getting, Meri had spotted telltale signs that Stella, her cleaning lady, was slipping. Stella had been with Meri from the beginning and was as fastidious as she was dependable. But she had just reached her eighth month of pregnancy and was finding it difficult to walk, much less clean tubs, toilets, and showers. Although Stella worked with an assistant, the latter was either late or absent much of the time. It would be simpler to hire a temporary replacement for Stella, but Meri knew Stella and her husband needed the money. Meri sighed. This meant she was going to have to help out with the cleaning. Besides doing the grocery shopping, scheduling, planning dinner parties, picking up dry cleaning, delivering meals . . . The list went on and on.

Where was she going to find help? she wondered. Bette was too busy chasing boys or sunbathing at the lake and wasn't interested in a part-time job. And Aggie . . . Meri sighed and smiled. Yes, Aggie was going to have to retire soon, bless her heart. Real soon. But not today, for goodness' sake. There just wasn't time!

"Guess who's moving in today?" Aggie asked as soon as Meri walked in the door.

Her heart skipped a beat. She didn't have to be told. "You're kidding."

Aggie shot Meri one of her familiar I-told-you-so looks. "He's gone back to his hotel to pick up another load. Said he'd be right back."

Chet Ambrose looked good in blue jeans, Meri decided instantly as she let him in the front door. He was carrying a stack of books under one arm. His other arm was bent, one finger looped through an assortment of clothes hangers from which business suits hung and were draped over his shoulder. His casual stance epitomized cocky self-confidence, a trait that Meri found strangely alluring. The work jeans gave sensual detail to the thigh and flank area, which was lean and slightly muscular.

"I see you didn't back out after all," she said, tearing her gaze away from his wide chest. It was covered by a form-fitting V-neck shirt and displayed a sprinkling of crisp curling hair.

"Did you think I would?" he asked smoothly.

She chose to ignore the question. "You needn't bother ringing the doorbell anymore . . . now that you . . . er, live here." She was still finding it hard to believe they would all be living under the same roof. "I'll have a key made for you first thing Monday."

"I can use the outside entrance to the apartment if you like."

"Suit yourself," she said, irritated with his conciliatory tone. "I'm not sure how dependable the steps are." She had forgotten how blue his eyes were. She started to walk away. "Oh, by the way," she said, turning back to him. "Aggie has cleaned the apartment and put fresh linens on the bed. There are clean towels in the bathroom. If you need anything, let one of us know. I'm usually out most of the day, but Aggie is here around the clock."

"Anything else, teacher?" he asked, grinning.

It was an effort to keep from smiling with him. "Dinner is usually at seven o'clock, or as near that time as possible," she continued. "If you're here for lunch, you'll have to fend for yourself. Aggie has other duties. We don't have time to give special treatment to anyone."

Chet dropped the smile. "Have I caught you on a bad day, Meri?" he asked politely.

She blinked. "Uh, no. I'm just setting the record straight."

"Good for you!" He nodded, apparently waiting for her to finish.

"Laundry is done three times a week, Monday, Wednesday, and Friday. If you have more laundry than that, you have personal problems." This, she saw, brought back the smile. "Any questions?"

"Would you have dinner with me?"

"Huh?" She wasn't prepared for that one. She inspected his eyes for a trace of humor, but found none. He was obviously serious. She glanced down at the floor.

"Did I miss your answer?" he asked.

"I've . . . er, already eaten."

He glanced at his watch. "But it's only two o'clock."

"I had a late lunch."

"Then we'll have a late dinner."

She looked up at him. "Why are you doing this?" she asked. "I mean, why are you inviting me to dinner?"

He didn't hesitate. "Because, number one, I want to have dinner with you. Number two, I think you would enjoy it, and three, I think Aggie would appreciate a night off from her cooking detail." His brow wrinkled in thought. "I can't think of any more reasons than that. However, you didn't specify how many I had to give."

She was tempted to accept. All his reasons made sense and she would have been lying had she denied wanting to go. She hadn't been out in months and, strangely enough, the thought of having dinner with Chet was a pleasant one. But . . . He was a client, she told herself. So? She'd had dinner with clients before. Yes, but this was different.

"Meri?" He leaned over to look at her face. "Do you want to go?"

She nodded.

"Then say yes. This stuff is getting heavy."

"Uh, yes."

He smiled and his eyes crinkled at the corners. "Is eight o'clock okay?"

"F-fine." She was still a bit dazed as she turned to go, and wondered if she should change her mind while there was still time.

"Oh, and Meri?"

"Yes?" She glanced around.

"Would you wear that dress . . . the red-and-blue thing with the scarf?"

She nodded dumbly, then walked on to the kitchen, where she found Aggie lurking behind the door and looking very pleased with herself, as if she'd just played a trump card.

Three

Dinner with Chet Ambrose was no casual thing, Meri thought as the maître d' ushered them through a maze of white-clothed tables and gleaming service carts laden with copper cookwear. She'd always wanted to eat at Aladdin's, a three-star restaurant that had been mentioned in all the culinary magazines as one of the finest in the Midwest.

Chet was right beside her, guiding her with his hand at the small of her back. She glanced around the room at the exquisitely dressed men and women sitting in high-backed velvet chairs. The walls were covered with a brocade of muted tones and the room was bathed in candlelight.

"Is this table to your liking, Mr. Ambrose?" the maître d' asked, his accented tones blending with the clinking of wine and water glasses.

"Perfect," Chet said.

Meri and Chet were seated, and before either of them had a chance to say anything, several waiters appeared, each with a certain task to perform. Water glasses were filled, a basket of bread and a plate of butter were set on the table. The maître d' stood stiffly in the background, alert for the slightest imperfection. "Would you care to see a wine list, Mr. Ambrose?" he asked, holding out a black book.

Chet was leaning on both elbows watching Meri, a curious half smile on his face. He didn't look up as he answered. "No. Just bring us a bottle of your best Cabernet."

The waiters, having finished their assigned duties, disappeared as quickly as they had come. "Amazing," Meri said, noting their efficiency.

"You're amazing," Chet said. "And very pretty. Thanks for wearing that dress."

She touched the collar of her dress self-consciously, surprised but delighted with the compliment. "You don't look so bad yourself," she said, and meant it. He wore a muslin-colored jacket that complemented nicely a pair of chocolate-brown slacks and dark beige shirt. All three colors were picked up in an expensive-looking tie. Chet thanked her, and she thought he looked genuinely pleased with her praise.

"Do you come here often?" she asked to keep the conversation rolling, even while she was trying to decide if she liked him better in blue jeans or in business suits.

"Not as often as I'd like." He was still leaning on his elbows, studying her boldly.

She squirmed under his stare. "I've heard the food is wonderful," she said, attempting to relax. "A couple of my clients have eaten here." The wine steward appeared and she was thankful for the distraction. She watched the man deftly open the bottle of wine with agile fingers and held out the cork to Chet for inspection.

"Go ahead and pour," Chet said, waving off the preliminaries. "I'm sure it's very good."

When both glasses had been filled and the bottle placed on the table, the steward left them to their drinks. Chet raised his glass in a toast, but waited until she had sipped from her own before putting his to his lips. "Glad you came?" he asked, setting his glass down.

"Yes," she said, glancing around the room. "I don't get out much."

"Except for work?"

"Except for work."

"Tell me about it," he prompted her.

"About my work?" she asked in surprise, wondering why he would be interested in something as dull as her job.

"Is it true you have twelve so-called husbands?"

No doubt he'd been talking to Aggie. She smiled. "Thirteen, counting you."

He looked pleasantly surprised. "That's right, I'm one of the guys now, huh?"

"The term *little boys* seems more appropriate at times," she said. "Present company excluded."

He nodded. "Why do you call them little boys?"

She liked his eyes best, she mused. They were warm and caring and at the same time intense. "Well . . ." She paused, trying to pull her thoughts together. That was difficult with him sitting across from her, watching her so closely. Thoughts just disappeared into thin air. "Each one of them has his own way of wanting things done," she began. "Each of them has his own likes and dislikes. It's hard to remember each tiny detail." She wondered if she would remember the details of Chet's face later. "But it's those details that mean so much to my clients," she continued. "They want to feel special. Sometimes it can be a bit overwhelming."

"Have you ever been in love with one of them?"

"Of course I love them," she said, smiling.

He cocked his head to the side and studied her as though trying to figure out whether she was serious or not. Meri thought he looked even more appealing as he did so. She sensed a certain vulnerability. "Really?" he asked.

"Not the kind of love a real husband and wife share, of course," she said quickly. "I feel a sort of protectiveness toward them, I guess." She shrugged. She'd never really questioned her feelings for any of her clients before. There was always too much work to do and not enough time in which to do it. "I want the best for them," she said slowly. "In their careers, their love lives, their homes. Of course, the only part I have any control over is their homes. I try to make them as comfortable as possible." She watched Chet's face as she talked and wondered if that was what she was feeling toward him, protective. She doubted it. There was something more, something she couldn't put her finger on. Was it attraction? That thought made her uneasy. "I guess I'm like a member of the family in a way," she said, trying to pick up the conversation where she'd left off. "Even if I could never mean as much to them as a real wife." She laughed self-consciously. "Does any of this make sense?"

"In other words, you're like a sister to them." He lifted one brow skeptically. "I'm sorry, Meri, but I find that hard to believe. I could never think of you as my sister."

She smiled. "Then think of me as your friend."

He leaned back in his chair and crossed his arms, giving her a somewhat quizzical look. "Don't you get tired of taking care of other people all the time? Who takes care of Meri Kincaid?"

"Meri Kincaid does," she answered simply.

"Don't you ever feel like letting someone else do it for a while?" he asked.

She dropped her gaze. "I had that once. For almost twelve years I let somebody else take care of me."

"And?"

"And when he died, I was devastated. And scared to death," she added, wondering why she was telling him this, why she was allowing him to pick her apart. "I didn't know the first thing about taking care of myself." She smiled, trying to make light of the subject. "In those days I believed I couldn't balance a checkbook if my life depended on it."

Chet studied her for a moment. "I can't imagine your being frightened by anything, Meri. You seem so capable and strong."

"I've come a long way in five years."

"You really like your job, don't you?" he asked. "I mean, it seems very important to you."

"It's been my whole life since Martin died," she answered. "I've learned to do things I never thought I'd be able to."

Chet smiled. "Like balancing a checkbook?"

"Among other things," she said, returning his smile.

He started to say something, but was interrupted by the appearance of their waiter, who handed them each a menu. Chet waited until the man left before asking, "Was it a happy marriage?"

Startled, she looked into his too perceptive eyes. That seemed a very personal question coming from one of her clients, a man she had known only for a week. But something about him inspired confidence, told her she could trust him. "I suppose it was happy," she finally said. "I was very young when I married. Only eighteen. Martin was twelve years older than I, a salesman from Kansas City. I was fresh out of high school and convinced I knew everything. The thought of spending the rest of my life working in a dime store in Polk City, Iowa, depressed me. When Martin proposed, I had no qualms about accepting."

"So you married him and moved to the big city, huh?" Chet said. He'd laid his menu down as though he were in no hurry to order.

Meri nodded, setting her own menu aside as well. "Bette was born a year later and I devoted my time to being a wife and mother." She shrugged. "Not many women had careers in those days. Anyway, Martin didn't approve of women working. He'd watched his mother work hard all her life and didn't want to see that happen to his wife." Meri smiled. "I know he thought he was doing the right thing, trying to protect me and all, but . . ." She paused. "I was so—so stagnant all those years. Sometimes I feel like I've got twelve years of living to catch up on." She looked down at the table. "I'm sorry," she said. "I didn't mean to bore you with the details of my life."

"You could never bore me, Meri," he said, taking one of her hands in his. He squeezed it. "You're one of the most exciting women I've ever met. And I'm not just saying that to make you feel good."

His hand was big and warm and comforting, while at the same time very disturbing. She tugged hers slightly and he let it go. "So what's next?" he asked, as if the moment of tension had never existed. "Now that you've conquered the business world?"

She laughed. "I don't think I've done quite that." She shrugged. "I wouldn't mind taking on more clients, but that would mean hiring extra personnel and I'm not sure that would be good for Wife, Inc. I don't want to be big and impersonal. My clients could just hire a maid service to get that. I guess I just want to be successful in what I do."

"And what's your opinion of success?"

She didn't have to stop and think of her answer. "Success means never having to be afraid to stand on your own two feet," she said. "I don't ever want to know that kind of fear again." She smiled, trying to lighten the intensity of the moment. "So now you know what makes Meri Kincaid tick."

A shadow fell over the table and she was surprised to see the waiter had returned. Neither of them had even looked at their menus.

"I suppose you're here to take our order," Chet said,

reaching for his menu. He looked at Meri. "Would you like for me to order for both of us?"

She nodded. "I'm sure you know what's good."

When the food started coming, Meri thought it would never stop. While they ate their appetizers, fettuccine in a thick cream sauce, Chet told her about his ideas for her house. By the time the waiter was preparing their Caesar salads beside their table, Meri was just as excited as Chet about his plans. There were leisurely pauses between each course, so they had plenty of time to talk. By the time the main course, veal Marsala, arrived, Meri didn't know how she was going to consume more food. But the veal was the most tender she'd ever tasted, cooked in a thick wine sauce, and when she laid her fork aside, she was surprised to see she had eaten almost all of it.

"No more food, please!" she said to the waiter when he rolled the dessert cart to their table. The cart was laden with Amaretto cheesecake, chocolate torte, eclairs, mousse, and various other delights. Chet declined as well and ordered coffee for both of them.

"I'm going to gain five pounds from this," Meri complained later as they left the impressive restaurant arm in arm.

"Don't worry," he assured her, helping her into his BMW. "We're going somewhere right now to work it off."

"I beg your pardon?" Meri asked.

"I thought we'd walk the Plaza," he said with wide-eyed innocence. "What did you think I meant, Meri?"

Chet kept her entertained as he drove them to the Country Club Plaza, guiding the car easily along a wide boulevard known as Ward Parkway. As always, Meri was awed by the century-old mansions that lined the boulevard. A median strip ran up the center of the boulevard. It was decorated with ornate fountains and flowers of every possible color. Orange and bright yellow marigolds were especially popular.

The Country Club Plaza was an exclusive area of shops, restaurants, and hotels, and was frequented by tourists as well as natives of the city. The entire area was done in a Spanish motif, adorned with tiles and lacelike grillwork, with some fifty objects of art, including twelve fountains.

Chet parallel-parked in front of an antiques shop. "Do you mind if I take my jacket off?" he asked. "I don't think I can handle these temperatures fully dressed."

"Go ahead," Meri said, wishing she could peel off some of her own clothes as well. She helped him slide his jacket off and draped it over the seat while he loosened his tie and pulled it off. "Why don't you roll your shirt-sleeves up?" she suggested, and without thinking reached over and unbuttoned the top button of his shirt. He glanced up at her and smiled. Meri, surprised by her own actions, jerked her hand away as though she'd just burned it. "I—I thought you'd be more comfortable."

He grinned as he rolled back his shirt-sleeves. "That's okay, Meri. You can undress me anytime you like."

A faint breeze cooled them slightly as they strolled along the wide shop-lined sidewalks, peering into the store windows. Chet linked his arm through Meri's as they walked, and she found her eyes invariably searching out his reflection in the glass as she window-shopped.

"I really like this place," he said. "I think this is one of the reasons I decided to sell my other stores first. So I could live here. It's nothing like Texas."

"Have you ever seen the Plaza during the holidays?" she asked.

"You mean the lights?" He shook his head. "I've seen postcards of it. Is it really pretty?"

"It looks like a fairyland," she said, smiling. "They

string up more than one hundred and fifty thousand lights."

He looked interested. "When do they turn them on?"

"On Thanksgiving." She laughed. "And every Thanksgiving the three of us climb into the car and fight the traffic to get here in time for the big event. Last year we had a hundred thousand people turn out for it. You can imagine how crowded it gets. And you can imagine how much Aggie complains."

He grinned. "You're right, I can imagine."

"And afterward she swears she'll never come back. But she's always the first one in the car when it's time to go the following year."

He threw his head back and laughed. "You'll have to let me come with you this year," he said. "It sounds like an experience I won't want to miss."

Meri's smile faded only a little. "Sure, you're welcome to come," she said. *If you're still here*, she added silently.

"Why don't we walk over to the park?" he suggested. His hand slid down her arm and captured hers, and although Meri tried to remain casual about the whole thing, her heart was thumping wildly in her chest. Chet led her across the street to where a tiny stream known as Brush Creek trickled through the center of the park. "Is it true this little thing actually flooded the Plaza a few years ago?" he asked, motioning to the rivulet.

Meri nodded solemnly. "And killed thirty people in the process. This whole area was underwater," she said, sweeping her hand around. "The flood did millions in damage." She pursed her lips. "It also flooded my basement."

He gazed at the stream in silence. "Looking at it now," he said, "one would never guess it could cause so much trouble."

She shrugged. "Like they say, things are not always what they seem."

He continued to hold her hand as he led her to the playground, where the swings and slides and seesaws looked eerie in the glow of the streetlamps. "People aren't always what they seem to be either," he said. "Do you think you are?"

She thought about that as she watched an elderly man collecting litter. "I don't know, Chet," she finally answered. "What kind of person do I seem to be?"

He glanced at her and smiled. "Harried."

She laughed. "Well, that's certainly true. Maybe that's why I don't know too much about myself. I haven't had time to find out."

"You work too hard, Meri," he said matter-of-factly.

She shrugged. "That may be true, but it's become a way of life for me."

They walked over to a wooden bench in the shadows of a giant oak, obscured partially by a row of tall hedges. He sat and pulled her down beside him, then slid his arm along the back of the bench, dropping his hand onto her shoulder.

"What would you do if you suddenly found out you had only six months to live?" he asked.

She was caught off guard by the question. "Six months?" She shook her head. "Gee, I don't know. It would take me at least that long to get caught up with work. I'd have to find someone to buy my business so Aggie and Bette could afford to live. I don't even like to think about it."

"I heard a story once about a group of cancer patients who were asked how they wanted to spend the rest of their lives." He smiled. "Not one of them said they wanted to spend the time working. They wanted to spend whatever time they had left with loved ones doing things they'd always wanted to do but never got around to because of their jobs or other obligations."

Meri winced. "Chet, that's the most depressing story I've ever heard. What have you been doing, studying the obituaries?"

He laughed. "I was only trying to make a point."

"The point being than you don't approve of my lifestyle, right?" She was tempted to tell him they were even because she didn't approve of his either, but she leaned back against the bench and clamped her mouth shut, determined not to spoil the evening. What did it matter if neither approved of the other? Chet had his life and she had hers, and even though they were going to be spending the next few months under the same roof, it didn't mean they had to agree on everything. All they had to do was fulfill their mutual obligations.

They were both silent, thinking their own thoughts, listening to the night as an array of sounds filled the air. Voices drifted from the tennis courts across the street as a ball slapped back and forth against rackets. A car backfired on the other side of the park, startling a group of teenage girls crossing the street in front of it. They shrieked, then seeing they were in no danger, fell into a fit of giggles. Both Meri and Chet laughed. When she looked up, she found his face close, silhouetted in the moonlight like a bronzed statue. His aftershave, although subtle, blended nicely with his own masculine scent, and she found it strangely alluring. She felt his hand tighten on her shoulder and saw the smile fade from his lips. He was going to kiss her, she thought as she watched his face come closer. And he did.

The kiss was light, a mere brushing of lips, lasting only a second or two. Meri felt disappointment when he lifted his head, but it was quickly alleviated as he shifted to try to make her more comfortable on the hard bench. His thoughtfulness warmed her as much as his embrace. He turned her around and pulled her back until she was reclining in his arms. *Then* he kissed her.

His mouth was warm, his breath clean and pleasant as he pressed his lips firmly against hers. It was a natural sort of kiss, one that conveyed friendship, affection, simple caring. It was not forced or practiced, nor was it meant to titillate or sweep her off her feet. It was special, in a category of its own. His grasp was firm and comforting, strong arms that enclosed her lovingly. Meri felt soft and womanly against his hard body, revered with the gentleness of his touch. He did not hurry. His mouth opened, slightly at first, as though not to frighten her, and his tongue slid back and forth across her bottom lip, tantalizingly slow, until her own lips parted and invited him inside. Once there, his tongue began a thorough, heart-fluttering exploration. Meri put her arms around his neck and drew him closer.

Chet's lovemaking, wonderful as it was, remained pleasantly unaggressive, and Meri was able to relax in his arms completely. His hand slid from her waist to her rib cage, halting respectfully beneath one breast. Never once did it trespass onto the soft mound, even as Meri ached for his touch. A wave of tenderness washed over her. Chet was offering only as much as he felt she was capable of taking. Knowing that made her more confident, less afraid. He was not going to rush her. He was leaving it up to her.

How long the kisses remained sweet and tender was a mystery to her. She lost track of time and wondered briefly what Aggie and Bette would think if she never returned home, if in fact she spent the rest of her life on this park bench with this delicious man. One minute she was snuggled cozily in his arms, and the next she was literally gasping with delight. Chet seemed to be traveling in the same direction. His breathing was labored. His lips became insistent and demanding, and his tongue plunged deeply into her mouth. His hands burned her wherever they touched.

Chet tore his mouth from hers and groaned. It sounded like it came from the very depths of his soul. "This is embarrassing at my age," he said, then laughed and buried his face in the softness of her hair. Until that moment Meri had not known how much control he'd been exercising. But she heard the frustration in his heavy sigh and saw that his fingers trembled when he touched her cheek. He had aroused in her feelings and emotions she had thought long dead. Her eyes burned with unshed tears as tenderness washed over her. She wanted to thank him while at the same time run away, but before she could say or do anything, he recaptured her lips in a final, desperate kiss.

"Sweet Meri," he said gently. "I think it's time I took you home."

Four

"May I ask you a personal question, Meri?" Chet asked as they drove home.

Meri, still a bit dazed from his kisses, nodded her reply even though she kept her face turned to her side window. "What is it?" she asked when he didn't speak right away.

"Have you . . . er, been with anybody other than your husband?"

She swung her head around in surprise. He was doing it again, she thought. Getting personal. "I've . . . dated here and there," she answered, being deliberately obtuse.

"That's not what I mean," he said, giving her a lazy half smile that told her he hadn't fallen for her dull-witted reply. "What I'm asking is whether or not you've made love with anyone since your husband's death. You don't have to answer if you don't want to." He paused and looked over her. "But I'd like to know."

"No." She turned back to the window.

"No what? No, you're not going to answer me, or no, you haven't made love with anyone?"

Her cheeks burned and she was thankful it was dark and he couldn't see. "I haven't . . . made love"— she swallowed—"with anyone."

"Haven't you thought about it?" he asked.

Her face grew even hotter. She could tell he was having difficulty concentrating on his driving. "Of course I've thought about it," she said a bit more tersely than she had planned.

"Then why—"

She snapped her head around. "Because I haven't met anyone I want . . . to be with, that's why." She was getting irritated with his line of questioning. "It's not like I have a lot of spare time to worry about something like that, you know. Not with my schedule."

"I'm sorry if I embarrassed you, Meri," he said, reaching over to pat her hand affectionately. "I just wanted to understand you better, that's all."

He sounded so sincere, she forgave him instantly. "In what way?"

He didn't answer for a minute. "I guess I'd like to know," he said finally, "why you have that look in your eyes all the time . . . that look of caution. I saw it back there when I kissed you." He shrugged. "I'd like to know why you get edgy sometimes when I ask too many questions or try to find out about you." He looked at her. "And I'd like to know why you insisted on paying for your own dinner."

"Chet—"

"Look, Meri, I'm not trying to get an FBI profile on you or anything like that. I just want to know you better. I told you earlier you interest me. I like you. I want to be your friend."

"I always pay for my dinner when I eat with a client," she said, knowing he wouldn't like that answer. Paying for her meal had seemed important at the time. Now she felt foolish. Perhaps it had been her way of pretending the evening was nothing more than a simple get-together with one of her clients.

When she dined with one of them to discuss the services she provided, more often than not she picked up the tab.

"I guess I was hoping we were on a more personal level," Chet said. He smiled at her, but the smile looked forced and didn't reach his eyes. "I don't think I like being thought of as just another client."

What could she say? Meri laid her head back against the seat and sighed. How could she tell Chet that she was feeling much the same way and that it frightened her? She'd never even considered getting personally involved with a client, especially one that would be sharing her house for the next few months. Or longer. There was no room in her life for involvement or commitment or any of the things that often came out of caring for another individual. And she would never again allow herself to be a mere extension of the man she loved. She was not the naive eighteen-year-old she had been, and she would never find happiness in that kind of life again. But . . . She glanced over at Chet and saw that he was staring straight ahead. She hated the disquiet that had settled over them. They were almost home and she didn't want to end the evening on a sour note.

"Chet, I'm sorry that I made such a big deal about paying for my dinner. And you do mean more to me than just another client." Her smile teased him. "After all, I'm trusting you with my house, aren't I? I would trust only a friend to do the things you're talking about doing to my home."

She knew that wasn't good enough and probably wasn't what he wanted to hear, but it was the best she could do. She should never have let him kiss her, that's where she'd gone wrong, she mused. He would naturally take it as encouragement when, in fact, she had only been caught up in the moment and for just a little while forgotten who she was and who he was and— Oh, well, she thought. Never mind what had already happened. She was going to have to discourage him, push the old friendship routine until he got the message.

He pulled into the driveway and parked next to her car. "Okay," he said, the old familiar smile returning, "I'll forgive you under one condition. That you'll come up to my place for coffee and dessert. I've got a frozen carrot cake thawing out. It should be ready by now."

"At this hour?" she asked in surprise, trying to see her wristwatch. But it was only a stall tactic. She couldn't have cared less about the time.

"It's not that late," he said. "Besides, tomorrow is Sunday and—" He looked at her suspiciously. "Don't tell me you work on Sunday too?"

"No, but . . ." Should she or shouldn't she? How would he take it? Would he see it as further encouragement? Perhaps she could use the time to undo what she'd allowed to happen earlier, make him see there could never be anything more between them than good old-fashioned friendship. She might even offer to fix him up with a woman friend of hers. "I guess I could come up for a few minutes," she said, and glanced at the house. No doubt Aggie was asleep. She herself wasn't ready to go to bed yet. The truth was, she was enjoying herself so much she hated to say good night.

Chet grinned and climbed out of the car, and before Meri could gather up her purse and do the same, he had her door open for her. He helped her out of the car. "Why don't we use the outside entrance?" he suggested, looking through his keys. "I want to see if this key Aggie gave me fits."

Meri followed him around to the back of the house, where a flight of sagging stairs led to the third floor apartment. They suddenly looked ominous to Meri. "I don't know how safe these stairs are, Chet." she said nervously, gnawing her bottom lip. "We'd better use the door."

"What's Aggie like if you accidentally wake her up?"

Meri shrugged. "She's a bear naturally, but I don't see—"

Chet took her hand and made his way toward the stairs. "I'd rather take my chances on these steps than risk going through the house and waking Aggie."

Meri laughed. "That's a terrible thing to say."

He looked up the tall flight of stairs. "Let me go first," he said, testing the banister. "Let's hope the stairs have held up better than the plumbing."

She watched him take a few tentative steps. The wooden steps creaked and groaned beneath his weight as he neared the halfway point, and she tried to remember when they'd last been used. She couldn't. Suddenly they swayed, leaning wickedly away from the house. The next thing she heard was a loud snap, followed by Chet's soft curse and her own shrill scream. Chet tried to scramble back down, but as he grabbed for the worthless banister, it gave way completely and his body was tossed to the ground. Fear welled up in her and rendered her motionless. The next thing she knew, Chet was sprawled out motionless before her.

He was dead, she thought in horror. She fell to her knees and began calling his name and shaking him. When he opened his eyes, she thought she'd collapse in relief. Nevertheless, there *was* something wrong with him. He tried to take a breath and couldn't. Meri felt helpless. She had never even taken a CPR class. If he died, it would be all her fault. Pinch the nose and blow into the mouth, she thought. Was that it? She tore at his shirt buttons—she'd seen someone do that before—and leaned over him, preparing to give him mouth-to-mouth resuscitation. All at once he made a wheezing sound, a strangled half cough, half gasp. He began to breathe.

"Are you okay?" she asked, her heart drumming

wildly in her chest. Perhaps he wasn't going to die after all.

"Knocked the . . . the wind . . . out of me," he said, trying to raise his head. "I think . . . I broke . . . my damn foot!"

The next thing either of them knew, they were bathed in light. The back door swung open and Aggie peered out, a large rolling pin held threateningly in one hand. "What in the name of heaven is going on out here?" she demanded, squinting at them in the darkness.

Next door at the Wilson house, the back porch light flashed on and Clyde Wilson emerged, wearing a checked bathrobe. "Everything okay over there?" he called from his back steps.

"Help me," Meri cried, motioning wildly to them. "I think Chet broke his foot." She began pulling off his shoe and sock, even as he protested in embarrassment.

"And just how in tarnation did he do that?" Aggie asked, stumbling across the backyard in her bare feet. "And what happened to the stairs?"

"Can you put pressure on that foot?" Clyde Wilson asked as he helped Chet up.

Chet's grunt was noncommittal.

"Help me get him to my car," Meri said, positioning herself under one of his arms.

"Meri, what are you doing?" Chet asked as she began urging him across the yard. "And where are you taking me in your car?"

"To the emergency room at the hospital," she answered, breathing heavily from the exertion. Clyde had joined in her efforts. "We need to have that foot x-rayed."

"No." Chet stopped moving. "No hospitals," he said flatly. "It's just sprained. If you could help me to the house." He tried to put his weight on the foot, but grimaced with pain and immediately lifted it.

"I think you should have someone look at it, son," Clyde said. "Look how it's beginning to swell."

"You're going to the hospital," Aggie said, "and that's all there is to it." She stalked ahead of them and pulled open the door to Meri's car. She looked at her daughter-in-law. "You want me to get dressed and go with you?"

Meri shook her head. "Don't bother. Once we get him inside the car I'll be able to handle things. I'm sure I can borrow a wheelchair at the hospital."

"I hate hospitals," Chet muttered.

But no one was listening. "Can you raise your leg?" Clyde asked, trying to get Chet seated in the front seat of Meri's car. "Lift your leg and swing it around. . . . Yeah, like that."

"Chet, do you need to prop your leg on something?" Meri asked, her voice calmer now. She was thankful her hysteria was beginning to subside.

"I'm fine," he mumbled, his jaw set in a hard line.

Aggie followed Meri around to the other side of the car. "Call me if you need me. I'll wait by the telephone."

"No, you go back to bed," Meri said, switching on the ignition. "I'm sure Chet will be fine." She saw that the lights had come on next door at the Blacks' house and both husband and wife were peering out their bedroom windows at the commotion. Clyde was still standing by the car as though wanting to make sure they got off safely. "Oh, and be sure to thank Mr. Wilson for his help," Meri added before backing out of the driveway.

"Something tells me using the back stairs wasn't such a good idea," Chet said once they were on their way. He tried to get his foot situated in the small car. "I'm sorry."

"I'm the one who's sorry," she said, pushing the accelerator against the floor. The car shot forward. "I should have had those stairs rebuilt a long time ago."

She sped past a stop sign without bothering to slow down.

Chet grabbed hold of his armrest. "Well, if you're worried about my suing you, don't. I've got better things in mind for you." He winced as the car bounced over a speed bump. "You really don't have to rush me to the hospital, you know," he said. "I mean, this is not exactly a life or death injury."

She gave him an innocent look. "I'm not rushing. Just sit tight and we'll be there in no time."

Meri frowned when she saw the crowded emergency room, where patients of every size and shape lined the walls, sitting in multicolored chairs of hard plastic. The black-and-white linoleum floor was waxed to a brilliance and the room smelled of disinfectant. She located an empty wheelchair and rolled it outside for Chet.

"Do we really have to go through with this?" he asked as though he were being led to the gallows.

"We've been through this a dozen times," she said, "and the answer is still yes. Try not to put any pressure on your foot," she added as he hopped from the car to the waiting chair. His ankle and foot had swelled to twice their size and had a nasty blue-and-purple tint. Once Chet was settled in the chair, she released the brake, grabbed both handles, and wheeled him through the automatic doors into the emergency room. Once there, they began the lengthy process of filling out various forms.

"There's no telling how long we'll have to wait," Meri said to Chet once they were settled in their seats.

He glanced around nervously at the other patients. An orderly had elevated his foot and covered the ankle with a disposable ice bag to prevent further swelling. "I warn you, Meri," he said, "if anybody comes close to me with a needle, I'm leaving."

She looked at him in surprise. He was clearly agitated. "They won't," she assured him. "All they're going to do is x-ray your foot and wrap it."

"Are you sure?"

"Positive."

He leaned back in his chair with relief. "Well, if I'm going to have to spend all night in a hospital, I can't think of anyone I'd rather spend it with." He smiled.

They emerged two hours later with Chet's foot securely wrapped in an Ace bandage and directions on how to care for it. It was after two o'clock in the morning when they pulled into the driveway back home.

"I guess this means you'll have to nurse me back to health," Chet said as he hobbled to the back door, one arm slung casually around Meri's shoulders.

"Correction. Aggie will." Meri unlocked the door and helped him inside.

"There goes all hope of TLC."

"Do you think you can get up the steps?" she asked, glancing hopelessly at the long staircase.

"Why don't I try hoisting myself up step by step in a sitting position?" he suggested.

"That'll take ages, but go ahead," she said, shaking her head. What a night. She checked the living room and found Aggie sleeping on the couch, the telephone on the floor beside her.

When Chet had managed to get himself up a few steps, Meri joined him. "Why don't you just sleep in my bed tonight?" she asked.

"Great idea," he said, grinning.

"And I'll sleep in Bette's room," she went on. "There's no sense in going up to your apartment. You'll never be able to get back down. You can just stay in my room until you're better."

Once Chet reached the second floor, Meri took over again and helped him into her bedroom. "Do I need to get you anything?" she asked once she got him to her bed. "A drink of water? Pajamas?"

"I don't wear pajamas."

"Oh." She tried not to let her imagination run astray at his remark. "You'll call me if you need anything?" she asked, backing away slowly from the bed.

"I could use your help getting undressed."

"I beg your pardon?"

"I don't think I can get my slacks over my bandage."

She stared at him for a full minute. "Is this for real?"

"Honest."

She sighed with frustration. "Okay, go ahead and take your pants off as far as you can. You *can* unbuckle your own belt and unzip your pants can't you?"

"Only if I have to," he answered.

She waited until he had unbuckled the belt and opened the fastening of his slacks. She refused to look directly into his face. "If you can ease the pants down past your hips, I'll be able to do the rest."

"Shouldn't we dim the lights or play soft music or something?" he asked, one corner of his mouth twitching into a smile.

She glared at him. "This is serious. If you want my help, you'd better cooperate."

"Or what?"

"Or I'll get Aggie in here to undress you."

"What do you want me to do?" he asked quickly.

"Get the pants past your hips." Meri continued to stare at the wall above his head, letting her gaze roam toward the ceiling then drop to the floor, anything to keep it off the man on her bed.

Chet unzipped his slacks and, balancing on one leg, managed to lift his hips from the bed and slide the pants down. "Okay, you'll have to take over from here."

There was no way for Meri to accomplish the task without looking at him. He sat very still as she grabbed the top of his slacks and pulled them toward his knees, trying to pry her gaze away from his lean but muscular thighs. She ached to touch them, to see if they were as hard as they looked. She tugged the pants past his knees and calves, aware that he was watching her. She tried several times to get the narrow leg opening past the thick Ace bandage, and at last succeeded. It would have been a heck of a lot easier, she thought, if her hands had not been trembling so much. She turned quickly from the bed and draped his slacks across a chair.

Chet unbuttoned his shirt and tossed it aside, completely undaunted as he sat almost naked before her, the exception being an Ace bandage and a pair of briefs. She sucked in her breath as she saw the masculine bulge that strained against the fabric. She felt her cheeks burn with embarrassment. "Could you help me under the covers?" he asked, amusement lurking in his eyes.

She tugged the bedspread and top sheet from under him and covered him as he lay down. She was unable to keep her gaze from straying to his chest and stomach, both of which were covered with wiry black hair. She had a sudden urge to press her face against his chest and inhale deeply the masculine fragrance that had teased her nostrils all night.

"They smell like you," he said, making himself comfortable.

She blinked. "What?"

"The sheets smell like you."

"Oh." She waited several seconds before she spoke. "Do you need anything else?" she asked, backing toward the door once more.

"I can't think of anything," he said. "But I feel guilty as heck taking your bed. We could always share, you know," he added, patting the spot beside him.

She gave him a benign smile. "You're so thoughtful, Chet. Another time, perhaps." She heard him groan and almost laughed out loud as she closed the door behind her. In Bette's room she peeled off her clothes and shoes, leaving them in an untidy pile on the floor. All she wanted to do was climb into bed and go to sleep. She pulled down the covers and fell onto the twin bed, trying to arrange herself into a comfortable position.

Sleep eluded her. Every time she closed her eyes she saw Chet lying on her bed, tan and lean. She tried counting backward from one hundred to distract herself, but couldn't manage it. She'd think of something funny he'd said at dinner or remember the way the moonlight had shone in his hair, or the way he looked in his underwear— Meri buried her head under a pillow. Why couldn't she keep her mind off the man's body, for goodness' sake?

"It's about time you got up," Aggie called from the breakfast room. She had the Sunday paper strewn across the table and her reading glasses were perched on the end of her nose. "Why didn't you wake me up when you got back from the hospital? And how come Chet is sleeping in your bed?"

Meri dragged herself into the kitchen toward the automatic coffeemaker, her bedroom slippers scuffling across the linoleum floor. She poured a cup of coffee and made her way into the small breakfast nook. "We didn't get back from the hospital until after two o'clock," she said, yawning. She fell onto a chair. "I told Chet he could have my room until his ankle gets better." She shrugged. "Anyway, Bette's gone for two weeks."

"Is he still sleeping?" Aggie asked as she scanned the sports section.

"Uh-huh. I just looked in on him." Thank heavens he'd been under the covers this time, she thought.

Aggie peered over the newspaper at her daughter-in-law. "Well, I can't begin to tell you how surprised I was to find him in your bed. A real eye-opener, you might say."

"I was just too tired to help him up another flight of stairs," Meri said sleepily.

"What's wrong with his foot?"

"It's his ankle. The doctor said he's got a severe sprain. He wanted to put a cast on it, but Chet refused. He's supposed to stay off it for at least a week, maybe longer."

"Oh, great. That's all we need around here, an invalid. Is he in pain?"

Meri shrugged. "The doctor gave him something to take if he starts hurting."

"Want to tell me about it?"

"About what?" Meri raised her coffee cup to her lips and sipped cautiously at the steaming beverage.

"About why Chet was climbing those good-for-nothing stairs in the first place," Aggie said, folding the newspaper and setting it aside.

Meri looked up at Aggie. "I'm not sure what you mean." As Aggie continued to stare at her, Meri began to understand. "Aggie!" she said, blushing. "Do you think we were . . . I mean, do you think I was going up there to . . . to . . ." She glanced over her shoulder to make sure they were alone. "It's not what you think," she whispered, a shocked look on her face.

"Oh? What do you think I'm thinking?"

"I know *exactly* what you're thinking. I can tell when your eyes get all beady that you're thinking the worst. I was just going up for dessert."

"Ah-ha!"

"Carrot cake and coffee," Meri insisted. She pursed her lips. "Believe it or not, it's the truth."

"I believe you," Aggie said grudgingly. "If I know you like I think I do."

"What's that supposed to mean?"

"Meaning you're so prudish and all—"

"I am not," Meri objected, truly offended. "I may not

be as . . . er, sophisticated as some women, but I'm not a prude. You forget, I have a daughter to raise."

The two women sat in silence for a moment. Meri finished her coffee, overcoming her grogginess at last. "I should never have gone out to dinner with Chet last night," she said, thinking out loud. "I should have listened to my instincts and said no. I think part of the reason I went was just to get my mind off business for a change. And for a while, I did. I felt different . . . young and alive and happy."

"And how do you feel this morning?"

She laughed. "This morning I feel like an idiot. The back staircase is lying all over the yard. I spent half the night in the emergency room, which by the way, cost seventy-two dollars, and on top of that, I've got an injured man sleeping in my bed. How do you think I feel?"

"Are you going to stop seeing him?"

"Stop seeing him? How can I stop seeing him when he's going to be living in the same house with me?"

"You know what I mean," Aggie said. "Are you going to stop seeing him on a personal basis?"

"I don't know." She looked up at Aggie. "What would you do?"

"I'd stop worrying about what's right or wrong or whether or not I had time and just follow my feelings."

Meri smiled. "I knew you'd say something like that."

Aggie took Meri's hand in hers. "Honey, let me tell you this. If a man like Chet Ambrose were to make a play for me . . ." She paused and rolled her eyes heavenward. "Well, frankly speaking, I wouldn't think twice about jumping in the sack with him."

"Aggie!" Meri was thoroughly shocked.

"That's right. And if you were smart, you'd do the same. You're not getting any younger, you know," she said, shaking a finger in Meri's face. She sat back in her chair and studied her daughter-in-law for a moment. "Yessiree, I'd go anywhere he asked me to go and I wouldn't stop after dessert and coffee." She leaned closer and whispered, "I'd let the man make love to me on a park bench if he wanted to. Yessiree!"

Five

"That hammering is driving me crazy!" Aggie announced the following Saturday as she and Meri discussed their work schedule at the breakfast table. "Can't that man find something else to do for a change? Something quieter?"

Meri looked up wearily from her papers, tucking a strand of blond hair behind her ear. August had never been so hot. Luckily Chet had repaired both air conditioners, but still it was all they could do to make the house tolerable against the heat wave. "I know," she said, loosing a bone-tired sigh. "But just think how nice it will be when he's finished."

"Well, if I had had to spend one more day doing his legwork, I would have moved out. Every time he wanted something, who do you think had to go find it for him? It's Aggie, get me those nails in the next room, or Aggie, would you find my screwdriver for me? Next thing I would have been fetching his slippers between my teeth."

"His ankle is much better now," Meri reminded her. "He's off the crutches and in another day or so he'll be good as new. And he's got that teenager helping him today. Remember, this was all your idea in the first place."

"That was before he busted his ankle and I became his personal servant," Aggie said.

"I know, I know," Meri said. There was no way she was going to confess having enjoyed the past week with Chet, despite his bad ankle. All his plans excited her, assuring her he was an expert in his field. It was a pleasure to arrive home at the end of the day to find he'd scraped and painted the frames of a whole room of windows while she'd been gone, or he'd put a new floor in one of the bathrooms. And there was something about the man in those tight-fitting jeans he wore when he worked. Thinking about it put a warm flush on her cheeks.

"Listen," she said, clearing her throat, while at the same time trying to clear her mind. "I've promised to drive Chet to one of his stores this afternoon while I run some errands. We'll probably be gone for two or three hours. Why don't you try to take a nap while we're out," she suggested, knowing Aggie's mood would improve if she rested. "I'm sorry I wasn't here more this week to help out, but I've been working with Stella. Poor girl can hardly walk, much less clean."

"Is she going to work right up till the baby is born?"

"She has to. Herb lost his job last month. The restaurant where he worked went out of business."

Aggie brightened. "That's right, he's a cook, isn't he?"

Meri nodded. "I know what you're thinking. I've considered hiring him to take your place, but where would he do the cooking? He can't use the kitchen on the third floor, since Chet's living in the apartment now; he can't use this kitchen because we're tripping over each other as it is. And he and Stella live in an apartment and don't have room there. You'll have to give me time to work on it." She patted Aggie's hand affectionately.

Aggie took on a look of martyrdom. "Well, don't worry about me," she said.

They were prevented from further conversation as Chet called out from the living room. Meri jumped from her chair. "Probably needs somebody to find his tape measure," Aggie grumbled. "I wish he'd lose that blasted hammer."

Meri found Chet standing on a ladder, trying to nail a strip of wood in place where he was replacing the old molding. He had a hammer tucked under one arm.

"Where's Barry?" she asked, referring to the teenage boy who'd been helping Chet.

"He had to run an errand at the store." Chet nodded to a second ladder standing right next to his. "Can you climb up there and hold this in place while I nail it in?" he asked.

She gulped. "Way up there?" she asked nervously. "You want me to climb up—up there?" She was getting dizzy just thinking about it.

"Yeah."

She hesitated. "You sure you don't want to wait for Barry to come back?"

"Yes, I'm sure. Could you please hurry? I'm getting a cramp in my arm from holding this."

Meri squared her shoulders and placed one foot tentatively on the bottom rung. She looked up at Chet. He seemed to be at least a mile up in the air. She began to climb slowly, one step at a time, willing herself to look straight ahead. She was eye-level with his belt buckle when her ladder wobbled. She gasped and reached out blindly for something to hang on to. She got the waistband of his jeans.

"Stop shaking the ladder," he said, "or you'll fall."

Meri didn't budge, couldn't budge. She was jolted to the soles of her feet that she had somehow managed to grab his underwear when she'd grabbed his

jeans, and her fingers were pressed against his flat
stomach. She could feel the crisp hair curling around
her fingers. Chet sucked in his breath and closed his
eyes as she accidentally jabbed him with a fingernail.
"Meri, what are you doing?" he asked, a bemused
look on his face.

"I'm—I'm terrified of heights!" she said in wide-
eyed horror.

"You're only five feet off the ground, for Pete's
sake."

"It . . . doesn't matter." She gulped. "It may as well
be fifty."

"Okay, what do you want me to do?"

"Don't move."

"Meri, we can't stay up here all day. Why don't you
just climb down?"

"I can't let go," she said, clutching the denim material so tightly that her knuckles turned white. She
pressed her face against his hard stomach, and his
old blue workshirt was smooth beneath her cheek.
His thighs were like concrete pressing against her
soft breasts, and although she would have been
mortified under normal circumstances, fear prevailed, and she found comfort in his warm strength.
Chet, on the other hand, had begun to perspire.

"Listen to me, Meri," he said, his voice quavering.
"We are both going to climb down at the same time.
Let me get rid of this strip of wood first." He set his
hammer down, then lowered his arms, balancing the
six-foot piece of wood in one hand. He let one end
swing around to the floor and dropped it on the thick
carpet. "Okay," he said as though talking to himself.
He laid his free hand on Meri's head and spoke gently.
"Meri, I want you to put your left foot on the rung
below your right foot," he said, "and I'm going to do
the same thing."

She shook her head, not daring to move.

"Yes, you can," he said, his voice taking on an air of

authority. "When I count to three, we'll both move our feet at the same time. You'll have to, Meri, or we'll both fall."

She nodded, still pressing her face against his stomach.

"One—two—three." They both moved one foot down to the next rung. "Good girl! See how easy that was?" he said. "Now, we do the same thing with the other foot. Stop shaking your head, Meri. You can do it, and before you know it, we'll be on the floor."

Meri did as she was told and almost collapsed with relief when her foot touched the floor. Chet took only a couple of seconds climbing the rest of the way down his ladder. "Are you okay?" he asked, grabbing her by the shoulders. "Your face is as white as your blouse."

Meri was humiliated and hid her face against his chest. "I'm sorry for being such a coward," she said. "I've never been able to stand heights. I think it's because I fell out of a tree when I was a kid and was badly hurt. I've been terrified ever since."

He held her tightly, stroking her hair. "It's okay," he said soothingly. "You should have told me. I would never have asked you to help me."

She looked up at him, comforted by his gentle tone. "I think that's why I became hysterical the night you fell from those stairs. I thought for sure you were dead." At the mention of his fall she glanced down at his feet in concern. "Did you hurt your ankle coming down the ladder?" she asked.

"My ankle is fine," he said, pressing his lips against her forehead. "I'm glad you care what happens to me."

Meri wasn't paying attention; she was fighting embarrassment. "I feel so stupid," she said. "You must think I'm a real loony bird."

"You mean because you're afraid of something?" he asked. He slipped a forefinger under her chin and raised her face to his. "Everybody is afraid of something, Meri. Each of us has our own demon to fight.

You're no different from the rest of the world." He smiled. "Other than being much prettier than everybody else."

She gazed into his eyes. His irises were bright blue specked with gold, surrounded by a darker blue ring that only heightened the rich color against the whites of his eyes. Yet, it was not the color of his eyes that captured her attention, but the emotions she read there, tenderness and concern and caring. "Are you afraid of anything, Chet?" she asked.

"Sure I am." He became serious. "I'm scared to death of the way I'm beginning to feel about you."

His face had come close, tantalizingly close, and his lips were only a heartbeat away. "Chet, please don't." His fingers massaged the back of her neck, drawing her closer, turning her legs to jelly.

"Don't what?" he asked, his eyes boring into hers. "Don't make you feel good?" His lips brushed hers like the silent flicker of a butterfly's wing.

It took every ounce of willpower she had to pull away. It had been like this all week, with them grabbing the odd moment to be alone together, to talk, to kiss. It had also been very frustrating. "I'm sorry, Chet," she said, "but I've got a million things to do this morning. I've got to meet with a client in less than one hour to discuss plans for a cocktail party, on top of picking up my schedules for next week." She saw his thick brows gather in a frown and ached to run her fingertips across them and smooth them out. "And I've got to pick up dry cleaning from four different locations, and—"

"Okay, I get the message," he said, sighing heavily. He ran a hand over his forehead, where beads of sweat had formed and started to run. "Can you still drop me by the store?"

"Can you be ready in twenty minutes?"

"I'll try." When she started to walk away, he grabbed

her hand and pulled her back. "One other thing. When are we going to have some time together?"

"Time together?" she repeated, blinking.

"Yes. To do something together besides look at wallpaper and paint samples."

"Gee, Chet, I don't know. This is a bad time for me with Stella scarcely able to work—and—"

"Just tell me when," he interrupted. "Surely you can spare a couple of hours for a friend."

"How about later this evening . . . or tomorrow afternoon?" She glanced at her wristwatch. "I really do need to be going. Can we discuss this later?"

Chet was dressed, sitting by the stairs, when Meri came down after having slipped into fresh clothes herself. Her gaze swept over him, taking in the tan slacks that emphasized his lean thighs. A crisp white shirt fell open at the collar, revealing dark curls she knew for certain ran across his chest, over his flat stomach, and . . . Well, never mind that, she told herself, glancing away on the pretense of looking for her keys. "Ready?" she asked lightly.

He stood up, still favoring his ankle. He could take the Ace bandage off permanently in a day or so, at which time he could go back to wearing his other shoe again instead of a slipper. "I'm ready," he said, walking to the front door and opening it for her. "You really don't have to drive me, you know. My ankle is much better. The only reason I asked you to drive me in the first place is so I could be with you."

She smiled at him, wondering if he was trying to turn macho on her. "I really don't mind driving you," she said, "as long as we can hurry. I'm supposed to meet my client in eighteen minutes."

"Eighteen minutes, huh?" He followed her down the sidewalk to the driveway. "That doesn't leave us much time to stop and smell the roses or anything like that."

"Don't bother getting my door," she said when he followed her. "Go ahead and get in."

"No. I insist on getting your door." He limped quickly to her door and pulled it open, and Meri laughed in spite of herself.

"I don't know what I'm going to do with you," she said when he'd joined her in the front seat. She started the car, jerked the gears into reverse, and squealed out of the driveway.

"Just pretend I'm a big teddy bear who needs lots of love," he said, grinning. He turned around and looked straight ahead. "Meri, do you see that stop sign—" He grabbed the dashboard with both hands. "Back there?" he finished, glancing over his shoulder at the passing sign. "No, I guess you didn't."

"Nobody ever drives down that street," she said, keeping her attention on the road in front of her.

"Thank heavens for that, huh?" He took a deep breath. "How come you're driving so fast?"

"Chet, I can't talk while I'm driving." She glanced at her wristwatch. "Just sit back and enjoy the ride, okay? I'm really running late today."

"Here we are," she announced fifteen minutes later as she pulled into the parking lot of the Handy-Andy Hardware and Building Supply. No small outfit, she thought, glancing at the oversize building. Both the remaining stores, Chet had told her, were replicas of those he had previously owned, and had sold off one by one and now offered franchises in other parts of the country.

A fenced area in back of both stores contained lumber and measured more than three acres. The interiors of the stores were about seventy-five thousand square feet in size and stocked every available tool known to hardware, as well as wallpaper, paint, kitchen and bathroom fixtures, doors of all kinds, even unique handmade breadboxes, canisters, and storage bins. It also housed larger items, such as unassembled utility sheds, patio furniture. Chet recited this information to Meri in the car while she drummed her fingers on the steering wheel.

"Chet, I'd really love to stay and hear more, but I'm late," she said.

"Aren't you even going to come in and see my office?" he asked, surprised.

She sighed, knowing it would hurt his feelings if she refused. "Okay, but I can't stay," she said, already climbing out of the car. "Five minutes. That's all."

"I didn't even want to come here in the first place," he grumbled, trying to catch up with her.

"You have no choice," she said. "They've been calling you for two days now."

He sighed and swung his arm around her shoulders. "I know. But I'd rather go somewhere with you and neck." He grinned. "I know this quiet little place—"

She laughed in spite of herself as he opened the glass door. They had managed to take only about three steps inside the store before Meri noticed the curious stares from the women at the cash registers.

Chet must have noticed it as well. He nodded and waved to the women, then leaned over to whisper into Meri's ear. "They're all wondering how I hurt my ankle," he said. "Think I should tell them how I was trying to slip you up to my apartment?"

"And compromise your flawless reputation?" she asked. She noticed the overly friendly smiles and looks a couple of the women were sending him, and was surprised by the feeling of sheer hostility that washed over her. "Perhaps you already have a reputation here," she added in a tone that would have turned warm water to ice.

"That's because I'm such a wonderful boss," he said, his mouth twitching at the corners. He frowned suddenly. "Lord, what a way to spend a Saturday afternoon."

They were prevented from further conversation as a balding man hurried toward them, his eyes darting nervously from Chet to Meri as he fastened a button on his jade-colored jacket.

"I'm glad you made it, Mr. Ambrose," he said. "The phone hasn't stopped ringing all morning."

"Meri Kincaid, meet Harold Walker," Chet said.

"Pleased to meet you, Mr. Walker," Meri said, offering her hand. He took it and pumped it, his tongue sliding back and forth across his bottom lip. She glanced at Chet. "I can see Mr. Walker is in a hurry," she began. "Maybe I should come back another time."

"No. I want you to see my office, maybe have a cup of coffee with me."

"Chet, I—" She wasn't able to finish her objection because Chet began pulling her toward the back of the store. Mr. Walker rushed ahead of them.

"Just one little cup of coffee," Chet whispered, "and I'll let you go." They entered his office, where Harold Walker was waiting for them. "Hey, Walker, is there any coffee?"

Mr. Walker shook his head. "The coffeepot died on us two days ago and I haven't had a chance to get another one. I can send out for a cup if you like."

"Don't we sell coffeepots here?" Chet asked, a bemused expression on his face.

"Yes. I'll take care of it right away. But first, I think you should see this." He picked up a large sheet of paper from the desk.

"Just a minute, Meri," Chet muttered, taking the sheet of paper.

"This is the last computer printout we ran before the computer went down," Mr. Walker said. "It shows an inventory of more than six hundred thousand pieces of lumber. But I've walked the yard myself and it's not there."

Chet studied the printout. "How long do they expect the computer to be down?"

Mr. Walker grunted. "Hell, they don't even know what's wrong with it." He glanced at Meri. "Pardon me, ma'am." He waited until she had nodded before continuing, his expression grave. "And that's not the only problem. Two of our top builders are threatening to sue if we don't deliver in forty-eight hours. We're already a week behind on their shipments." He pointed accusingly at the printout. "According to that, we have it in stock. But I know we don't. There's not enough lumber out there to fill one order, much less two."

"Who signed for the lumber?" Chet asked.

"McIntosh." Mr. Walker searched through a stack of papers on the desk. "Here are the bills of lading. Fifteen boxcars. And there's his signature."

"Okay, I'll talk to McIntosh. You start calling the other stores and see if they can help us out. Call our competitors if you have to."

"They're not going to make us a very good deal."

"Then we'll take a loss." Chet tossed the computer printout aside. "And let me know exactly what those builders have coming to them."

Meri glanced at her watch for the umpteeth time. "Chet, I really have to be going—"

"I'm sorry, Meri," he said, throwing his hands up in frustration. "This place is a zoo. Next time I'll have coffee and doughnuts for you, how's that sound?" He walked her to the door as Mr. Walker began dialing a number on the telephone.

"It's okay," she assured him.

"I know," he said, brightening. "Why don't we have lunch together? How long are you going to be tied up this morning?"

"Two or three hours."

"Why don't you bring us back a couple of hamburgers then?" He reached into his back pocket for his wallet and pulled out a handful of bills.

"I've got it," she said, shoving his hand away. Chet

was prevented from saying anything further on the subject as Mr. Walker asked him a question. Meri slipped through the door and fled.

She returned more than three hours later, hot and tired and bearing two sacks of food. Chet was nowhere to be found. As she was searching through the store, she ran into Harold Walker. "Mr. Ambrose is out in the yard taking inventory," he said before she could question him. He smiled shyly. "We're in a bit of a mess."

Meri nodded her understanding. "In that case," she said, rearranging the food in the sacks, "would you just pass this on to him. I'll run on home and wait for him to call me to come pick him up."

"That won't be necessary," Mr. Walker said. "I'll be more than happy to drop him off myself. There's no telling how long this is going to take."

Chet did not return home until after midnight. Meri, who had fallen asleep on the sofa watching a late movie, was wakened by the sound of a car door being slammed. She hurried to the front door and pulled it open easily, thankful it had been one of the first repairs Chet had made. Chet was standing on the other side, searching through his key ring for his key. "You look beat," she said, noticing the white lines around his eyes and mouth.

"I am," he said tonelessly, dragging into the living room. He slumped into the nearest chair.

"Are you hungry?" She could tell he wasn't in a good mood.

"No. I had a cold hamburger a couple of hours ago."

She sat on the couch across from him, her heart going out to him. What had ever made her think the man lacked ambition? It was obvious he was a hard worker. "You really do look tired, Chet," she said.

"Why don't you go to bed? You can sleep late tomorrow."

He sighed and leaned his head back. "I've got to go in for a while. Walker's picking me up at eight o'clock."

"On Sunday?" she asked in surprise.

"We're doing physical inventory. It's going to take forever to get it done." He rubbed his eyes and yawned. "On top of that, I've got to have the books ready for my lawyers to go over on Monday."

"Oh?"

"Yeah. Somebody is actually interested in buying the place, I think. Both stores, as a matter of fact. They aren't talking about as much money as I'd asked, but it's worth it to me to get rid of the headaches."

"You mean you still want to sell?" she asked.

"Of course I do." He raised his head and looked at her. "Does that surprise you?"

She shifted on the couch. "Well, I guess I thought you'd changed your mind. You never mentioned it again, and when I watched you this afternoon, you seemed . . . you seemed to handle things so well. As if you were in total control of the situation."

"That doesn't mean I like doing it."

"What about my house?" she asked anxiously. "And your brochure?"

"I'll still be able to work on your house."

"And how much is it going to cost me?" It was a hard question to ask, but she had to know. The look on his face told her he didn't appreciate it.

"I've already told you there's no charge. I'm doing it in return for room and board. I'll simply have more time to work on it if the stores sell."

"Then what?"

"What am I going to do when I finish your house?" he asked. He shrugged. "Find another one, I suppose.

I'll worry about that when the time comes." He gave her a hard look. "Why are you asking?"

She laughed. "I guess I'm surprised a successful businessman like yourself would be content to putter around an old house." She smiled at him like she would at a naughty child. "You just wait, Chet," she said, waving her finger at him. "You'll be bored to death in six months."

"Why do you say that?"

"Because you won't be using your full potential, that's why. I know what I'm talking about, Chet. Remember, I've been there. I spent ten long years doing nothing. A person needs to be challenged, needs to be—"

"Look, Meri," he said quietly, his jaw set in a hard line. "I don't tell you how to run your life and I don't appreciate your telling me how to run mine."

Her mouth fell open in surprise. "I'm not telling you how to run your life, Chet. I'm merely offering my suggestions—"

"Don't."

"Somebody needs to stop you from throwing your life away."

"Throwing my life away? Is that what you think I'm doing?" He looked surprised. And angry. "What do you know about life, Meri? You don't have time for it."

"What's that supposed to mean?"

He sat forward in his chair. "Meaning you're a workaholic, Meri, that's what. It's as simple as that."

"A workaholic?" she shrieked in disbelief.

"That's right. You let work dictate your life. You don't take time for what's important. Like your relationship, for instance."

"What relationship?" She snorted. "The only relationship you and I have is business."

"Oh, yeah? Do you kiss on park benches with all your clients?" he asked. "No wonder your business is booming."

Meri clenched both hands until her nails threatened to puncture her palms. He was laughing at her. She ached to slap the smile right off his face. "That sounds like something you'd say. Not only do you lack ambition, you lack manners."

"What do you mean, I lack ambition?" he said, jumping up from the chair. "I had to be pretty ambitious or I would have never begun working on this place. And I think I've done more than just putter around, as you say, considering the mess it was in when I started."

"What mess?" she demanded. She glanced around the room, wishing they had not picked that particular room in which to argue. It needed more work than the others. "I was doing fine before you moved in. Anyway, why do I need a man to tell me how to decorate my own house?"

"Lady, anybody who would paint their breakfast room red, white, and blue definitely needs help."

"What's wrong with those colors?" she asked, madder than fire because he'd brought it up. "I happen to like them."

"Oh, nothing is wrong with them," he said, each syllable ringing with sarcasm. He shrugged. "I suppose you could always rent it out for the next Republican convention."

Her breasts heaved in anger. How dare he make fun of her house, he who could afford luxury housing and the finest hotels? "If you don't like this place, you're welcome to leave immediately. Tonight! I won't even charge you room and board for the time you've already spent here."

"Room and board!" He threw his head back and laughed. "Are you serious? Who's going to pay me for all the work I've done? Who's going to reimburse me for putting new locks on your doors and windows?"

"I never asked you to do that. I thought you were just going to throw some paint on the walls."

"No, you didn't ask me. You wouldn't part with your precious money to have it done. You'd rather risk having someone break into this place and rob you." He glanced around the room. "But then, any thief would take one look and see everything you own is falling apart."

Meri crossed her arms and squeezed her fists. What she'd give to pop him right in the mouth! Pride held out. She refused to let him know he'd gotten to her. "Perhaps I can't afford to buy the best," she said, lifting her chin proudly, "or afford to hire decorators to see that it's done tastefully. So I—I do the best I can." Her eyes burned with unshed tears. "Why do you think I work so hard?" She hadn't realized she was yelling until she'd stopped.

Chet rubbed his hands over his face. "Let's just drop it, okay. We've both said enough."

"And maybe I *do* spend a lot of time working," she continued as though she hadn't heard him. "But that's because I can't afford to hire dozens of people to do the work for me." She saw his face darken and knew she'd hit a nerve. She should stop now. Before someone got hurt. But she couldn't help herself. "I think you're just jealous of my work, Chet. Because I derive such pleasure from it . . . and personal satisfaction. I won't give up my work so that I can devote all my time to you, live in your shadow."

Meri regretted her words the instant she said them, but it was too late. Chet stared at her in disbelief, his eyes cold and hard. The silence was deafening. When he finally spoke, his words were clipped and without emotion. "I believe you've confused me with someone else, Meri. Martin is dead. If you screw up the next twelve years of your life, it's going to be all *your* fault." He turned and, still favoring his hurt ankle, stalked across the living room to the stairs. "I'll sleep in my own bed tonight," he said, never looking back as he spoke.

An hour later Meri was still trying to strip her bedroom of Chet's presence. Even after the sheets had been changed, the bathroom scoured, and his personal items relocated to a box in the hall, the clinging scent of his aftershave haunted her.

Chet spent most of the following day at the store and arrived home shortly before dinner. He was cool and distant, concentrating on his food. Then, instead of remaining downstairs to chat as he usually did, he went upstairs without a word. Leave it to Aggie to notice.

"I don't know which is worse," she grumbled, stacking the dinner dishes into the dishwasher, "the two of you trying to slip off to be together all the time or carrying on like angry roosters. Either way, you're making me a nervous wreck!"

Meri was thoroughly depressed. By the time she had prepared for bed that night, she had decided on a solution to the problem. She would ask Chet to leave, to get the hell out of her house and life forever. She sighed, slipping between the cool sheets. She was beginning to sound just like Aggie these days.

Six

The following week was difficult for Meri, both in her work and at home. Leaving the house much earlier than usual, she tried to complete as many of her own tasks as possible before she joined forces with Stella, whose assistant had not bothered showing up for the past three days. Meri swore she'd fire the girl on sight if she ever saw her again. Although Aggie had put a help-wanted ad in the newspaper, Meri had no idea when she would have time to interview someone.

She had not asked Chet to leave as she had planned, and he hadn't made things easy by offering to move out. When he began to take the entire house apart, she backed off. There was no way she and Aggie could tackle the job alone, and they couldn't afford to pay for the kinds of changes Chet planned to make. For the time being, Chet Ambrose was going to stay.

Renovation was in full swing. The carpet in both the living room and dining room had been pulled up and Chet was in the process of sanding both wood floors. Grit was everywhere. The furniture was covered in old sheets and dropcloths to protect it, and the draperies had come down as well, giving the downstairs a barren, oppressive atmosphere. Meri thought it suited her mood perfectly. But whatever else she may have thought of Chet since their argument, she could not condemn his work habits. Everything was done carefully and professionally.

Chet and Meri seldom spoke except to discuss some phase of the work, such as which stain she preferred or what color she wanted a certain room painted. More often than not she found herself following Chet's suggestions, not because she wanted to get back in his good graces but because he always seemed to know what enhanced each area. Although they were polite to each other, they created a fog of tension that one couldn't help noticing. Bette was aware of it as soon as she returned home the following weekend.

"Is somebody around here mad?" she asked before she'd even unpacked her bags.

Aggie gave a disgruntled snort, ignoring Meri's look of warning. "It depends on the day of the week, honey," she said. "You just never know what to expect in this place."

Chet's aloofness did not extend to the rest of the family, Meri noticed. He always seemed to be around whenever Aggie needed him, whether to take out the garbage or make a simple repair. He was the doting Dutch uncle for Bette, patiently listening to her problems, which more often than not centered on the opposite sex.

Only hours after Bette's return Meri heard them discussing pictures in a fashion magazine. Bette was forever trying to imitate the models' use of makeup, and her efforts, at their best, were overkill. "You don't need all that garbage on your face," Chet said, examining the pages in the magazine. "Men don't like having to look through a glob of mascara to see into a woman's eyes."

"Really?" Bette seemed to cling to every syllable.

"Would I lie to you?" he asked, his tone sincere. "Men like a fresh clean look on a woman—clean face, shiny hair."

Meri slipped away quietly, shaking her head. How many times had she told Bette that same thing? But let Chet Ambrose say it and it might as well be carved in granite.

On Monday morning Meri walked downstairs before six o'clock to make coffee. Thinking she would be alone, she hadn't bothered with a robe and walked into the kitchen wearing a pale blue nightshirt. She flipped on the light, and gasped when she saw Chet leaning against the kitchen cabinet with a cup of coffee in his hand. He gave her an apologetic look. "I didn't mean to startle you. Want to join me for a cup of coffee?"

The smile she gave him was forced. Her pulse beat erratically as he poured her a cup and handed it to her. "Thanks," she said as she took the cup, wishing her hands weren't trembling so badly. She stood rooted to the floor, wondering if she should go back upstairs and put on her robe. She hated to be obvious though. She looked up at Chet and found him watching her. She guessed he'd just stepped out of the shower. His hair was damp, and he smelled of soap and aftershave. He wore faded jeans that had undoubtedly seen more washings than her coffeepot, and a blue workshirt open at the collar, displaying part of his chest. Meri resisted the impulse to run her hands across that chest and watch its hair curl around her fingers like silken rings.

"How have you been?" he asked with polite formality.

"Fine. And you?"

One corner of his mouth lifted in a smile. "I'm okay."

She groped for something else to say. The silence hung between them like a thick curtain. The coffee-maker made a burping sound that caused both of them to smile. Until that moment Meri had not realized how much she'd missed seeing his eyes light up when he smiled. "What would you say to calling a truce?" he asked.

She didn't answer right away. Her heart was thumping wildly in her chest and she took a deep breath, hoping to slow it down before it gave her away. She licked her lips nervously and watched his gaze follow the gesture. "A truce?" she repeated.

He nodded. "I mean, just because we don't always see things eye-to-eye . . ." He shrugged. "We shouldn't allow something like that to ruin our friendship. And as long as we're going to live under the same roof . . ."

Meri pondered the idea, turning it over and over in her mind, examining it like a small child who'd just found an interesting new toy. "You're probably right," she finally said. "I'm sure Aggie and Bette would appreciate it."

"It's not just that, Meri," he said, jamming his hands into his pockets. "I've missed you. It's no fun doing all this work if there's nobody to share the pleasure. Aggie couldn't care less what I do to this place." He grinned, a teasing glint in his eye. "And it would make things easier on you as well. That way you won't have to come sneaking down to the kitchen before six o'clock every morning just to avoid running into me." He cocked his head to the side and a damp curl fell over his forehead.

Meri blushed. "Are there no secrets in this house?" She ached to take that curl between her fingers and pull it gently, just to see if it would spring back into place. He was right, of course, she thought. They should try to get along, if not for themselves then for the sake of the others. She smiled, realizing she hadn't smiled in days. He must have taken it as a sign of acquiescence, because his own expression grew hopeful.

He offered his hand. "Friends?"

She took his hand and shook it, marveling at the warmth and strength of it. She saw him wince and jerked her hand away. "What is it?" she asked.

He shrugged. "Nothing really. I got a splinter in my thumb the other day and I can't seem to get it out. It's kind of sore."

She reached for his hand and looked at his thumb where the splinter had buried itself. "No wonder it's sore," she said. "It looks infected."

"It'll be okay."

"Aren't you going to do anything about it?" she asked, touching the red place with a fingertip.

"What do you suggest?"

"You need to get the splinter out, silly." She let go of his hand and crossed the kitchen, then pulled a box out of one of the cabinets.

"What's that?" he asked.

"My first aid kit." She set it on the counter and began digging through it, placing several items near the sink. "Come over here and let me wash that," she said, glancing at him from over her shoulder.

He didn't budge. "Why?"

"Because I'm going to try to get the splinter out and I want to make sure your hand is clean."

"Of course my hand is clean. I just took a shower. And my thumb is just fine the way it is." He took a step backward, holding his hand behind him.

Meri shook her head at him. "Would you please get over here and let me wash your hand?"

"Is it going to hurt?" He moved toward her slowly, still undecided.

"No." She grabbed his hand and held it under the warm water as she squirted dish soap on his thumb.

She ran her finger over the splinter and lathered it, and he winced as though in great pain. She dried the sore area with a small square of gauze.

"Now what are you going to do?" he asked when she picked up a small plastic bottle of alcohol.

"Clean it with alcohol."

"Why?"

She couldn't help the laugh that bubbled up from her throat. "Would you please stand still and stop asking so many questions?" She opened the bottle, moistened a cotton ball, and dabbed the splinter with the antispetic.

Chet sighed when she let go of his hand. "That didn't hurt a bit," he said, walking away.

"That's because we're not finished yet," she said, her lips twitching at the corners. She reached into her box and pulled out a small box containing a razor blade and two needles.

"What is that!" Chet took one giant step backward.

Meri lit a kitchen match and basked the needle in the tiny blue flame. "We're going to have to take the splinter out, Chet," she said matter-of-factly. She blew out the match.

"Like hell we are."

She arched one brow. "Do you want it to become infected?" she asked, and watched him pale at the thought. It took every ounce of willpower to keep a straight face. "Or worse, have it amputated?"

"Amputated?"

"Suit yourself," she said, turning her back on him.

"Wait!" She glanced over her shoulder at him. "What do you have to do?"

"Pick the splinter out with this needle."

"Will it hurt?" He held his hand at a protective distance.

"You won't even feel it."

He looked sheepish. "I hate needles. The only thing I hate worse than needles is blood. My blood."

"You don't have to watch."

"Can I sit down?"

"Chet, this is not major surgery. I'm only going to remove a splinter."

"I'd feel better if I were sitting."

She sighed heavily. "Okay." She began picking up her supplies. "Let's go into the breakfast room." She led the way and pulled out a chair for him. "Sit down."

"Now, you're sure this won't hurt?"

"Positive. Just look the other way until I'm finished." She took his thumb and held it securely in one hand. Then, without hesitating, she touched the exposed tip of the splinter with the needle. Chet winced. She continued probing until she was able to get a firm hold of the splinter, then she pulled it out. "Okay," she said, and saw his shoulders sag in relief. "I just have to put this Band-Aid on it." She picked up a small Band-Aid and wrapped it around his thumb. "All finished," she announced.

Chet turned hesitantly in his chair and looked at his thumb as though expecting it to have been dismembered. "Oh, that wasn't so bad," he said. He stood up. "Thanks, nurse. Now, what do I get for being such a good boy?"

She felt her face grow warm. "Sorry, I'm fresh out of lollipops."

"I was thinking of something just as sweet but with fewer calories," he said, smiling enticingly.

Meri looked away, pretending to busy herself with cleaning up. She felt more than saw him move closer, and her entire body tingled. She looked up and he was only an inch away. She sucked in her breath and held it as he captured her chin with his hand and lifted her face upward. Her heart seemed to explode as his lips touched hers. Then, almost reluctantly, he pulled away and the look in his eyes took her breath away. She looked down self-consciously, wadding the gauze in her hand. "I've got to take a shower," she said breathlessly, "and get out of here." She could still feel his mouth on hers, smell the lingering scent of his aftershave.

"What's the hurry?" he asked in a caressing tone that made her stomach flutter. Before she knew what was happening, his arm was snaking around her waist. He pulled her into his arms, and she could feel the rough texture of his jeans through the gauzy material of her nightshirt. His belt buckle pressed against her stomach, and his lips pressed against hers. He coaxed her mouth open with his tongue and the kiss deepened. Her head swam, her legs threatening to fold under her. This couldn't be happening, she told herself over and over again. But it was happening, right in the breakfast room. She knew she should put a stop to it, but she didn't have the strength. Where was her willpower when she needed it? At last Chet released her.

"I'll let you go, now," he said, as though trying to convince himself as well as her. But when she started to move away, he captured her hand and stopped her. "By the way," he added, grinning, "I like your nightie. When the light hits it just right, I can see every gorgeous curve of your body."

An hour later, showered and fully dressed, Meri stood at Bette's door and knocked. There was a muffled sound in response, and a few seconds later the door opened. Bette, her hair hanging in her face, stared at her mother sleepily.

"I need your help," Meri said. "That assistant called yesterday and quit and I haven't hired anyone else yet. I'll pay you minimum wage if you'll help me clean for a few days."

After much complaint Bette emerged from her bedroom wearing cutoffs and a T-shirt. "I had planned to go shopping with LaDonna," she grumbled, following her mother out to the car.

"That takes money," Meri said, sliding into the driver's seat. "Besides, don't you get tired of borrowing Aggie's car all the time? You should be thinking of buying one for yourself." She cranked the engine and spun out of the driveway.

"I have been," Bette said, clutching the door handle.

"Then you'd better think about earning some money. Cars don't come free, you know."

"LaDonna has a car and she doesn't work."

"LaDonna is spoiled rotten."

"Oh, Motherrr!"

"Work never hurt anybody."

Bette made a grimace and slid down into the seat to prevent the early morning sun from spilling into her eyes. "Not everybody thrives on work like you do," she muttered, stretching languidly. "You act like there's nothing in life but work, work, work."

Meri frowned at her daughter. Bette was beginning to sound like Chet. "It pays the bills," she said succinctly, "and I haven't heard you complain about that."

Bette shrugged, then leaned against the door and studied her mother as if seeing her for the first time. "Mom, are you in love with Chet?"

Meri almost ran a red light. Bette might as well have asked if she and Chet had ever made love in the backyard, such was the extent of her embarrassment. A crimson blush stained her cheeks. "What on earch prompted you to ask such a question?" A horn tooted behind her, reminding her the light had turned green. She eased the car onto the main street, glancing over at her daughter tentatively.

Bette was smiling. "You'll have to admit he *is* awfully sexy."

"What do you know about sexy, young lady?"

"I wasn't born yesterday."

"Oh, yes." Meri nodded. "You're a mature woman of

sixteen now, aren't you?" There was gentle teasing in her voice.

"I'm exactly two years younger than you were when you married Dad."

Meri winced. "Don't remind me. I was too young to know what I was doing."

"Well," Bette said somewhat loftily, "I happen to know a few things about sex, and I can tell Chet has the hots for you."

"Bette!"

"It's true. You should see the way he watches you." She giggled. "Especially when you're walking out of the room. He watches the way your butt wiggles."

"Oh, good grief!" Meri exclaimed, the blush spreading to the tips of her ears. "He does not." She turned her attention back to the road, trying to concentrate on her driving, which at this point had taken second place in her thoughts. After a moment she asked, "Does he really?"

Bette nodded. "Uh-huh." She gave her mother a woman-to-woman look. "You should be pleased, you know. At your age it might not be a bad idea to start thinking about settling down."

To Meri's surprise and delight, Bette was a good worker, complaining very little about the menial tasks she had to do. It was agreed that Bette would do the dusting and vacuuming while Meri went about the more serious task of scrubbing.

By the end of the first day they had cleaned three apartments. By Wednesday they had covered six apartments and two houses while Stella worked in another section of the city. On Thursday Meri left Bette to clean an apartment by herself while she ran errands, delivered dry cleaning, and picked up various grocery items. Although she didn't buy extensive amounts of food, part of her service was to replenish empty refrigerators and cabinets.

From time to time she was expected to help with dinner or cocktail parties, for which she and Aggie prepared and served the food themselves. If the party was to be extravagant, Meri called on a good friend in the catering business. But at all times Meri was present to oversee the work, and sometimes even played hostess if there wasn't a girlfriend or secretary to do so.

Over breakfast on Friday Meri gave Bette the day off, paying her in full for the four days she'd worked. "Spend the day at the lake," she suggested, "or go shopping. Thanks to you, Stella and I are getting caught up. It's up to you if you want to work next week."

"I really don't mind working today if you need me," Bette said, looking long and hard at her paycheck.

Meri smiled. From the corner of her eye she saw Chet standing in the kitchen doorway listening to their conversation. She smoothed down her full pale blue skirt self-consciously. She had not had the opportunity to see him alone all week, and wondered if he'd thought about the kiss as much as she had. "Go ahead and take the day off, kid," she said to her daughter. "You can always come back to the salt mines next week."

Bette grinned, waving her good-morning to Chet. "Oh, well, I guess the lake *does* sound better than cleaning furniture all day." She gave her mother a peck of a kiss and left.

Meri and Chet watched her race up the stairs in an unladylike fashion. Chet winked at the girl and strolled casually to Meri. "Your daughter is growing up," he said, smiling over the rim of his coffee cup. He took a sip of the steaming beverage, watching her, his eyes no longer cool and aloof, but friendly. "I read somewhere that it's a sure sign of maturity when a teenager begins thinking of someone other than him- or herself."

"I'll have to admit it's refreshing," she answered, studying him from under long lashes. Even in workclothes he was a striking figure of a man. His self-confidence was subtle yet powerful, letting her know he was at all times sure of himself and the situation. He could talk on any subject, she thought, whether it be politics, current affairs, sports, or even the weather outside. "Well," she said somewhat breathlessly, "I guess it's that time. Duty calls, as they say." She wanted to stay, wished that he would ask her to stay to share another cup of coffee. She would have done it gladly. But he didn't ask.

"I guess it *is* that time," he agreed, glancing at his watch. His gaze returned to her face, lingering at her lips, and she was certain by the look on his face he would have kissed her had Bette not come running back down the stairs. When he spoke again, the tenderness in his voice played havoc with her nervous system. "Have a good day, Meri," he said, the corners of his mouth lifting into a smile. "I'll be thinking of you."

Meri drove toward Country Club Plaza and the elite section of town, where one of her clients, Harvey Bright, lived. Harvey was a prominent criminal lawyer who, although divorced several years, had never gotten over the need to have a woman care for him. He was Meri's toughest client. When she arrived at the elegant Tudor-style house, she saw Stella's car already parked in the driveway. They planned to clean the house together and prepare for a cocktail party for that evening. Aggie was supposed to drop off the food in the afternoon. Meri entered the house and called out for Stella.

"You look terrible," she said the instant she laid eyes on her.

Stella, a slightly plump woman in her late thirties,

sat at the kitchen table drinking coffee out of the plastic cup from her thermos. She looked quite miserable. "Thanks," she said. "That's just what pregnant women love to hear." She motioned to the chair beside her. "Come have a cup of coffee with me."

Meri grabbed a cup from one of the cabinets and joined Stella, still eyeing her suspiciously. "What's wrong? Don't you feel well?"

Stella shoved her thermos toward Meri. "I didn't get much sleep last night. It's getting harder and harder to get comfortable." She pointed to her protruding belly.

Meri shook her head. "I don't see how you manage to walk," she said. "Why don't you try to take a nap this afternoon? We're pretty well caught up, thanks to Bette."

"How is Bette?" Stella asked.

"Oh, you know, sixteen going on thirty."

Stella laughed, then winced, grabbing her side. "It's nothing," she said, seeing the startled look on Meri's face. "A stitch in my side, that's all."

"Are you sure you're all right?" She didn't wait for the woman to answer. "I'm worried about you, Stella," she said frankly. "You should be in bed eating pickles and ice cream, not working like this."

"Sure. So I can just lie in bed and stare at the ceiling all day and wonder when this kid is going to come. No thanks. I'd rather keep busy."

"Has the doctor given you any idea when we can expect to see this little sweetie?" Meri asked, patting Stella's stomach.

She shrugged. "A couple of weeks . . . or three. What does he know? I've called him twice this week complaining of labor pains, but he told me to lie down and see if they would go away. They did."

Meri shook her head. "Well, hopefully I'll have a replacement for you soon. You need to stop working and stay home until this baby comes."

"I could always get down on my hands and knees and scrub floors or something," Stella said, smiling mischievously. "Maybe it would start labor."

"Don't you dare!" Meri exclaimed, shaking a finger in her face. "You're not going to get *me* involved in delivering a baby. I'm warning you, Stella, I'm no good in emergencies."

"There's nothing to it," Stella said. "Do you know how long it took me to have Jeremy?" she asked, referring to her four-year-old son. "Exactly forty-five minutes from start to finish."

"Good grief! It takes me longer than that to pick out something to wear in the morning."

Stella and Meri had a second cup of coffee while Meri ran a load of towels in the washing machine. She had Stella do light dusting while the first load dried, then parked her on the couch in front of the television set to fold clothes while the second load dried. The two women worked at a relaxed pace, chatting occasionally, and Meri felt confident for the first time in weeks that everything was under control.

When she carried the second load of laundry into the family room, she found Stella sleeping on the couch, her hands folded protectively over her large stomach. She smiled, switched off the TV, and closed the door so she wouldn't wake her up when she vacuumed. By lunchtime Meri had the house in order and was beginning to wonder where Aggie was. She was relieved when the doorbell rang, but when she opened the door, Chet—not Aggie—was standing there with the box of food.

"Hi," he said. "I talked Aggie into making extra so we could have some for lunch."

Meri smiled and shushed him, explaining that Stella was in the next room sleeping. "Bring it into the kitchen," she said, pointing him in that direction. "It sure smells good."

He grinned. "It *is* good. I personally sampled each

item, from the goose liver pâté to the smoked salmon and the stuffed mushrooms. But I like the ham and Swiss cheese biscuits best, so I asked Aggie to make up an extra plate for us." He set the box down on the kitchen table and held up the plate. "Ta-da!"

"I'm surprised you talked her into it."

"You won't believe what all I had to promise to do in return. I've got to take the garbage out every night for the next two weeks, plus wash her car and wax it, not to mention—"

"Oh, but it was worth it," Meri said, biting into one of the biscuits. "They're delicious." She began to unload the box of food, putting several items in the refrigerator.

"I've got a couple of more boxes out in the car," Chet said. "Don't forget to save some of those biscuits for the little mama in the next room."

As though on cue, Stella suddenly cried out from the next room. Meri and Chet exchanged nervous glances and hurried to the door. Meri threw it open and gasped in disbelief. Stella was lying sideways on the couch, her feet tucked under her, her hands clutching her abdomen.

"What is it?" Meri asked frantically, not wanting to believe her eyes.

"My water just broke!" Stella cried. "I think the baby is coming!"

Shock rendered Meri speechless for a moment, and she thought her knees would buckle under her. She spun around and faced Chet. "What are we going to do!" she demanded. "I don't know the first thing about delivering babies. What if—" She broke off, trying to get a grip on herself.

Chet grabbed her by the shoulders and shook her. "Calm down," he ordered in an authoritative voice. "Women have babies all the time. It's no big deal."

"No big deal!" she shrieked. "No big deal!"

"Would you stop getting hysterical, for Pete's sake! I only meant that she wasn't likely to die from it."

"Would one of you please call an ambulance?" Stella asked in a meek voice.

Meri and Chet both looked at her as though they had forgotten her for a moment. Chet nodded. "Right!" He hurried through the door, then turned around and came back. "Where's the telephone?"

"On the kitchen wall by the refrigerator," Meri said over her shoulder. "Stella, you sit tight while I get clean towels and sheets. And shouldn't I boil water?" she asked, stopping at the door.

"What for?" Stella croaked.

"I'm not sure. People always do it." She shrugged and ran out the door. "Oh, well, we'll skip that part for now."

Five minutes later Meri had Stella stripped from the waist down and wrapped in a clean sheet. Stella was just going into another contraction when Chet rushed in with a wet washcloth. Meri wiped the woman's brow as the contraction intensified and Stella cried out, clutching her belly.

"Don't tense your body like that, Stella," Meri said. "Try to take a few deep breaths . . . and relax." She looked at Chet. "How long since you called the ambulance?"

"Seven minutes," he said.

"Listen to me," Meri said, mopping perspiration from the woman's brow. "Let me know when you feel another contraction coming on. We'll try to breathe or count together and see if it goes any easier." Meri had no sooner gotten the words out of her mouth before the next one hit. "Let me help you this time, Stella. Take a deep breath." Chet offered to time the contractions while Meri worked on the breathing routine with Stella. As the seconds ticked away, the contractions worsened, making concentration difficult for the laboring woman.

"Just a few more seconds and it'll be over," Chet said. "Come on, Stella. You can do it."

"I don't think we have much time, folks," Stella cried. "I think—" She was interrupted by the ringing of the telephone.

"Want me to get it?" Chet asked. "It might be Aggie checking to see if I found this place okay." Meri nodded and he hastened through the door. A few seconds later Meri heard him answer the phone.

"I don't think the ambulance is going to make it in time," Stella said, grasping Meri's hand tightly.

"Just try to hang in there, Stella. They should be here any minute."

"Harvey Bright is on the phone," Chet said, sticking his head through the doorway. "He wants to know if he can invite three more people to the cocktail party and can they come at five-thirty instead of six-thirty?"

"I feel another contraction coming," Stella said.

"Oh, great!" Meri said "That's all we need." She saw Stella flinch. "Not you, Stella. I was talking to Chet."

"That's not all," Chet said, giving Meri a sympathetic look. "He says to tell you his bartender canceled on him. He wants to know if you can find somebody to fill in."

"Just tell him yes to everything!" Meri said, throwing her hands up in frustration. "I can't worry about that right now. Tell him I'm busy and can't come to the phone." She glanced over her shoulder at Chet. "Don't mention anything about Stella having a baby on his couch." He nodded and raced out of the room.

Stella let out a low wail that almost caused Meri to fall off the couch. "I can't stand it any longer," Stella cried. "I want to go home!"

"No, Stella," Meri said frantically. "You can't go anywhere." She raised the sheet up slightly and froze.

"What's wrong?" Chet asked from the doorway as though afraid to come in.

"The baby is coming!"

He gulped. "You mean . . . now?"

"I've got to push!" Stella cried, raising her head up.

"No, don't!" Meri ordered. "Take a deep breath, do anything, but don't push!" The look she gave Chet was almost pathetic. "Please help me!"

He hesitated for only a second, but something in Meri's eyes must have convinced him she was desperate. He hurried into the room and leaned over Stella. "Look at me, Stella," he said, taking a deep breath. "Do what I do." He glanced at Meri. "Are you sure this is what I'm supposed to do?"

Meri looked up. "Did you hear that? I think I just heard a siren." All three listened for a moment.

"It *is* a siren," Chet said, looking immensely relieved. He rushed out of the room.

"Did you hear that, Stella?" Meri said, grinning. "The ambulance is almost here. Just take another breath . . . short ones will do fine. That's right, keep it up. In and out. In and out."

"I have to push!" Stella yelled. "I have to!"

"Just a few more seconds," Meri said, taking her hand and squeezing it. She wiped the woman's face again. "They're just down the street. I hear Chet yelling like a complete idiot, so they must be close."

"It's too late!"

Meri held both of Stella's hands so tightly that she was afraid she would cut the poor woman's circulation off. She heard the siren, coming closer and closer until she feared the ambulance would slam right through the walls of the house. But it stopped and the next sound she heard was Chet's booming voice ordering everybody into the house. The front door opened and slammed and a herd of footsteps sounded in the living room. When they reached the door to the family room, all three men came to a respectful halt and stared in disbelief.

"Come in, gentlemen," Meri said, smiling proudly.

Her eyes were bright with tears. "Come meet Stella's brand new baby boy." She gazed down at the infant who lay on a clean sheet draped across her mother's belly.

Chet was the first to enter and walked across the room like a sleepwalker. The two paramedics were right behind him. Chet stared at the infant as he craned his red and wrinkled neck and wailed loudly, telling the onlookers how hungry he was. Everybody laughed. Almost everybody.

Chet's eyes rolled back in his head, and he fainted.

Seven

"Don't you dare laugh at me!" Chet warned from the bed, peering out at Meri from beneath a damp washcloth.

Despite her lips' temptation to curl upward into a smile, Meri managed to keep a straight face and swallow whatever remnants of humor she might have found in the situation. Looking at the scowling face before her, she was briefly reminded of how the matador must feel right before the bull charges him. Nevertheless, there was something almost vulnerable about Chet right now, all six feet two inches of him sprawled out on the bed. She cleared her throat. "What makes you think I'd laugh at you, for goodness' sake?" she asked, as though the thought had never crossed her mind. But his eyes narrowed slightly and told her she had done nothing to alleviate his suspicion.

"And if you get any ideas about telling Aggie or Bette about this," he said, "I'll never speak to you again!"

"Tell them what? That you fainted?"

"I did *not* faint," he said indignantly, jerking himself upright on the bed. "Not exactly," he added. He threw his legs over the side and shoved his feet into his shoes. "I merely got . . . er, light-headed. Can I help it if the paramedics made a big deal out of it?" He tossed the washcloth onto the floor.

Meri retrieved it. "You're the one making the big deal out of it," she said, glaring at him. His jaw was rigid, his bushy brows knotted together in a fierce frown. But it was his eyes that told the real story. He wasn't angry, Meri realized. He was embarrassed. That knowledge made her want to take him in her arms and soothe his troubles away.

She knelt before him on the thick carpet and placed her palms on his kneecaps. He started, and for a split-second she saw the raw need in his eyes before he frowned again, putting the grim mask back into place. She edged closer, squeezing her slender body between his thighs, and without giving it a second thought slipped her arms around his lean waist and locked her fingers together behind him. He sucked in his breath and looked down at her in surprise, and she was reminded once more how nice his eyes were. But they were troubled now too. No doubt his male ego was blasting him for his moment of weakness, and she would have done anything to make him understand how much more she cared for him because of those feelings. How refreshing it was to know a man with a softer side, one who could show strength and dominance as well as compassion and tenderness. One who could be all things. That, compounded by his very potent kisses, was an alluring combination. How could she make him understand that it was okay to have feelings? She sighed. She might as well try to describe a sunset to a blind man.

For a moment they were silent, even as Chet relaxed against her and draped his arms over her shoulders. "I feel so dumb," he finally said.

Meri didn't budge. Her face was tilted up, her eyes staring directly into his. "Why?"

He answered with an indifferent shrug, but his eyes clouded, letting her know he cared very much. "I let you down," he said. "I pretended there was nothing to it . . . to having a baby—" He took a deep breath. "But in the end I failed you."

She frowned. "How did you fail me?" she asked in disbelief. "I couldn't have done it without you."

He tore his gaze away, looking past her as though he couldn't face her with the truth. "By passing out like that. I wanted to be strong for you, to let you think I could handle it. But then, when it was all over and—and I looked down at that tiny creature . . ."

"You didn't let me down," she said, her eyes misting once more. Suddenly she laughed. "Good grief, I haven't stopped crying since it happened. And my legs feel like jelly. I was scared to death. If it hadn't all happened so fast, I wouldn't have been able to go through with it." She lowered her head, letting it fall against Chet's thigh. She felt one of his hands touch the top of her head tentatively, as though wanting to soothe her as well, offer whatever he could to help her for the moment.

He surprised her with a soft chuckle. "We're like two dogs licking each other's wounds," he said, and she laughed as well. "The next time I tell you having a baby is no big deal—"

"I'll kick you," she interrupted with a loving threat. She turned her face to his and offered her lips to seal the promise. He took her mouth in a kiss that left them both shaking afterward.

He cupped her face in his hands. "Meri, you don't plan on having more children, do you?" He didn't wait for her to answer. "I mean, I couldn't stand it if you had to go through all that pain."

She was warmed to her toes by his thoughtfulness, but couldn't help smiling at the serious look on his face. "No, I don't plan to have any children in the near future," she answered. "It *is* uncomfortable having a baby, but when it's all over and you see the baby for the first time, it's worth it."

"Did it hurt when you had Bette?" he asked, a frown wrinkling his forehead.

"I'm sure it did, but that was sixteen years ago. It's hard to remember just how it felt."

"Was your . . . was Martin with you at the time?"

She shook her head. "Bette was two weeks early. Neither of us suspected she would come that soon. Martin was away on business."

"Who was with you?" he asked with concern.

"My parents came up the next day from Iowa."

"You mean you went through all that pain alone?"

"There were nurses and doctors there," she said, smiling. "I had a very sweet nurse who held my hand the entire time."

"If you had been *my* wife I would never have left you," he said fervidly. "I would have stayed by your side the whole time, throughout the pregnancy, right up to the time the baby came." He dropped his gaze. "Even if it meant getting sick or passing out."

"That's very sweet, Chet, but I don't think either of us has to worry about that happening. What I *do* have to worry about—"she pulled herself up from the floor—"is getting this place ready for a cocktail party."

Chet stood as well. "What do you want me to do?"

"Go home. You've helped enough."

He shook his head. "I'm not about to leave you alone with all this work to do, not after what you've been through. Anyway, you need somebody to play bartender for you tonight, remember?"

She slapped her hand against her forehead. "Damn, I'd forgotten."

"I'll be able to tend bar as long as they don't order anything fancy."

She shook her head. "They won't. The usual mixed drinks, wine, or beer. I've already checked the bar and it's fully stocked, so it shouldn't be any trouble. Chet, are you sure you don't mind doing this? I mean, this is my responsibility and all—"

"I want to help you," he said, pulling her into his arms. "Maybe when all this is over and you're caught up, we can spend some time together."

She sighed, letting her head fall against his chest. "It sounds wonderful. When I get caught up." And when would that be? she wondered.

Harvey Bright walked through the door at five-fifteen. Meri and Chet were ready and waiting, having spent the past few hours cleaning and preparing the rest of the food. Chet had vacuumed the entire house while Meri finished cleaning, and now it was spotless. "Clean enough to entertain the President of the United States," she had declared, giving the house a final scrutiny.

"Everything looks wonderful," Harvey said as he shook hands with Chet, whom Meri had introduced as merely the bartender. "You're a gem, Meri." He put his arm around her shoulders and squeezed her affectionately. "I don't know what I'd do without you. Why don't you give up all those other men and marry me for real?" he asked, his eyes twinkling.

Meri laughed. Slightly overweight, Harvey reminded her of a cocker spaniel, with his big brown eyes and docile personality. He released her and took her hand, leading her around the table of food, sampling the various hors d'oeuvres and asking questions. Harvey was a toucher, she knew. Men, women, children—it didn't matter. He was very demonstrative with his feelings. A strange trait for a criminal lawyer, she thought, someone who obviously spent much of his time concealing his true thoughts and feelings. "Mind if I try this?" he asked, dipping a cracker into clam dip. "Mmmm, you and Aggie have done it again. It all tastes delicious."

"Would you excuse me?" she asked. "I need to check everything once more before the guests arrive." He let her go, content for the time being to hang around the table and taste everything. Meri checked the living room and den to make sure there were plenty of ashtrays and that Chet had found everything he would need for the bar. Everything was perfect. She smiled. Nobody would ever suspect a woman had given birth there only a few hours earlier. She wondered how Stella and the baby were doing. She hadn't had a chance to call the hospital, although she had gotten in touch with Stella's husband, Herb, and informed him. She was certain he would make sure Stella had all she needed.

The guests started arriving shortly after five-thirty, and by six o'clock there were at least twenty people there, members of the bar association, Harvey had told her. They planned to have cocktails at Harvey's and go on to dinner at the Plaza. Meri was thankful she didn't have to serve a sit-down dinner for this many people. Especially after the kind of day she'd had. She was beat. And from the looks of it, so was Chet. Besides mixing and pouring drinks, he'd made routine checks to empty the ashtrays and refill the bowls of popcorn and peanuts in the two rooms. It was all Meri could do just to keep the food coming. She watched him as she set out more crackers. He hadn't smiled all night.

"Oh, Meri," Harvey called out, motioning for her. "Come over here, Meri. I want you to meet some of my friends." She hurried over to where Harvey stood talking to several men. He took her arm and made the introductions. "This is the woman I've been telling you about," he said, placing his hand at the small of her back. "Isn't she great? Oh, stop blushing, Meri," he said, giving her a fatherly hug. "You know it's the truth." Meri shook hands with the men as best she could with Harvey holding on to her.

"Are you really a surrogate wife of sorts?" an older gentleman asked. He was a district court judge.

Meri nodded. "Of sorts," she said, smiling.

"She does everything," Harvey said proudly. "She buys my food, cooks it, cleans my house, does my laundry. You name it." Another firm squeeze. "She even goes shopping with me and picks out my clothes. And the great thing about it"—he grinned at her—"if we split up, I don't have to pay alimony." The men roared with laughter and Meri pretended to give Harvey a dirty look. Harvey didn't make a secret of the fact that his former wives had all tried to wipe him out financially.

"I'd love to hire your services," the older man said, stroking his snarled gray beard. "Every since my wife, Effie, died, I can't seem to find anything. I can't get organized. I've got a housekeeper that comes in twice a week, but she's as lost as I am."

Meri smiled at him. How many times had she heard that same story? The world was full of lonely people. "I'm sorry, Judge Hoffman, but I'm not taking on new clients at the moment. I'll be happy to give you a call when there's an opening." She waited while he wrote his telephone number on a piece of paper and handed it to her. "Now, if you gentlemen will excuse me, I have to check on the food." She hurried over to the table once more, and for the next thirty minutes made sure the guests had all they needed. When she checked the time, she saw there was only twenty more minutes before they had to leave for their eight o'clock dinner reservation. Thank goodness, she thought. She was running out of food. If the guests left on time, she could get the place cleaned up and be out by nine o'clock. She glanced over at Chet and decided to see if she could help him with anything.

"How are you doing?" she asked, coming up behind him.

He shrugged. "Okay, I guess." He took a damp cloth from a shelf and began to clean the bar.

Her smile faded when she saw the distant look in his eyes. "Is something wrong?" she asked, coming closer.

"You might say that." His tone was cold, and when he faced her, so were his eyes. "I'm tired of watching that creep put his hands all over you."

"Chet!" She grabbed his arm and led him into the kitchen. "Somebody will hear you," she said in a heated whisper. "Do you want to see me lose one of my best clients?"

He shrugged. "Do you want to see me toss a drink in his face?"

She planted her hands on her hips and glared at him. "You wouldn't dare!"

His jaw was hard. "Don't tempt me, Meri."

They faced each other in a standoff, and from the look on his face Meri began to think he might go through with it. "Chet, I can't believe you're making such a big deal out of this. That's just the way Harv is." She had never seen Chet so angry.

"Harv?" he repeated. "Is that the little nickname you've given him?" He crossed his arms. "I had no idea you were so . . . friendly with your clients."

She stared at him for a full minute, trying to understand the reason for his anger. Suddenly it hit her and she smiled. "Chet Ambrose, you're jealous," she said.

He pulled himself up to his full height. "I am not!"

"You are so."

"Am not."

"Are so."

He glowered at her. "Okay, so what if I am? Just because you work for him, that doesn't mean he should be able to climb all over you."

"He was *not* climbing all over me. Anyway, what gives *you* the right to talk? You've done a lot more than put your arms around me and I've known you for only a few weeks."

"That's different."

"Oh? How so?"

"Because, I—" He paused and looked directly into her eyes as he spoke. "Because I care for you. I think I'm falling in love with you."

Meri was jolted into silence. She stared at him in surprise, her ears ringing. Could Chet really be falling in love with her? Harvey picked that particular moment to push the kitchen door open and stick his head in.

"Meri, we're leaving," he said, throwing her a kiss. "Thanks for everything, hon. And thank Aggie for me." He waved at Chet. "I appreciate your covering the bar for me. Just send me the bill." He left and the door swung shut behind him.

The silence in the kitchen was unbearable. Meri shook her head and held her hands out. "Chet, I had no idea—"

"Then you're blind."

"That's not fair," she said. "You know this has been a bad time for me. What with Stella the way she's been and the other girl quitting . . ." She hesitated. "And after that fight we had, we've barely seen each other."

"Why do you think I'm here tonight?" he asked, moving slowly toward her. "I came over this afternoon to ask you if you'd have dinner with me tonight. Of course, I had no idea we'd have to deliver a baby and throw a cocktail party in the meantime. So much for that idea." He sighed heavily and looked at her. "So you tell me . . . when *is* it going to be a good time for you? When are you going to have time for me?"

"Chet, I'd love to have dinner with you tonight," she said, taking a step closer. She slipped her arms around his waist. "Let's not fight. We've only just become friends again."

"We're more than friends," he said. "When are you going to face it?"

"Do we have to talk about this right now?" she asked. "You know I never meant for things to go this far between us. Believe me, I never meant to encourage you."

"Why did you let me kiss you?"

She dropped her arms to her sides. That was a question she'd asked herself a dozen times. "Because it felt so nice, that's why," she said. "Haven't you ever just wanted somebody to hold you, Chet? Haven't you ever needed to feel loved or desired? Do you know how long it has been since anyone held me close . . . or tried to love me?" She felt the sting of tears behind her eyelids. Why was she telling him this? And why couldn't she stop crying, for heaven's sake? "With you, it's different. You're a man, you can do whatever you choose, whether it be a permanent relationship or a one-night stand."

He shrugged. "So can you."

She gave a snort. "Yeah, I wish. I don't have the guts for it, Chet. I've thought about it, believe me. You'd be surprised the things I've thought about doing. In the beginning, right after Martin died, I got so lonely, I thought I'd die."

"So what did you do?"

"I buried myself in my work," she answered simply. "I found out that if I climbed into bed exhausted, I wouldn't lie awake and cry, or wish I had somebody to hold me until I fell asleep." She laughed. "You call me a workaholic. I call it survival."

His expression was tender as he pulled her into his arms. "You don't ever have to be alone again, Meri," he said gently. "You've got me."

"I know. That's what scares me."

"You don't have to be afraid of me. I'm not going to

hurt you. I merely want to love you. Why don't you stop thinking and worrying and rationalizing and just take things as they come . . . one step at a time."

"That's difficult for me," she said. "I like knowing what's ahead."

"Life isn't always that simple, Meri," he said, one corner of his mouth lifting into a smile. "Life is full of bumpy roads, swift turns, and surprises. You of all people should know that." He tucked her head under his chin and held her close, stroking her hair as he talked. She felt her insides melt. "That's why it's important to live each moment to the fullest, as though it were your last." He leaned back and grinned down at her. "Why don't we get this place cleaned up and go have some fun?"

She laughed at the boyish look on his face. "What kind of fun?" she asked suspiciously. Suddenly she wasn't tired anymore.

He shrugged. "I don't know. We could grab something to eat and go bowling."

"I don't know how to bowl, Chet."

"Don't know how to bowl? That's un-American. I'll have to teach you." He snapped his fingers. "I know, we can go roller skating."

"Roller skating!" She laughed. "I've haven't done that since I was twelve years old."

"Look, Meri. Some things you never forget. It's like making love. Once you know how—"

"Chet, I don't think I want to hear this," she said, a blush spreading across her face. "I don't think I could skate across this room without breaking my neck."

"There's always the drive-in movies," he said, rubbing his hands together like he was about to enjoy a delectable feast. "We could park in the back row and neck." His bushy eyebrows slid up and down in an imitation of Groucho Marx.

"No thanks. I think I'd better take my chances in the roller rink instead of the backseat of your car."

She glanced at her skirt and blouse. "Shouldn't I run home and change first?"

"Naw, you'll be okay. I won't let you fall down."

"Okay, then we'd better get this place cleaned up. Why don't you start bringing the dirty dishes in and I'll load the dishwasher and clean the kitchen."

"Right."

"And don't let me forget to call the hospital and check on Stella, as well as call Aggie and tell her we're going to be home late."

"Yes, teacher."

Thirty minutes later they left the house, having cleaned up and made the necessary phone calls. "I told Stella I'd come by the hospital and see her first thing in the morning," Meri said. "She told me to thank you for everything and she hopes you didn't hurt your head too badly when you fell."

"Must we go back over that?" Chet muttered.

"What should we do with my car?" Meri asked, having forgotten they had two cars there in the first place.

"Leave it for now. We can get it on the way home." He helped her into his car, then climbed in on the other side. "Okay, where do you want to eat? There's a family restaurant down the main highway that serves home-cooked meals and has a salad bar. I know you prefer junk food, but I thought this once you might eat a decent meal."

"I don't eat that much junk food," she said, giving him a hurt look.

He threw his head back and laughed. "You're talking to me, Meri, remember? The man who sits across from you at the breakfast table. I've seen you eat cold pizza for breakfast. You're a junk-food junkie if ever there was one."

"Okay, let's go to your family restaurant," she grumbled.

"You're going to thank me for this one day," he

said, as he drove to the restaurant. "For teaching you all these healthful habits." He reached over and patted her hand affectionately.

She sighed. "The next thing you'll be doing is trying to get me hooked on your vitamins," she said.

"That's a good idea." He smiled. "Why didn't I think of that?"

"Chet, I've never taken a vitamin in my life except when I was pregnant, and I'm in perfect health. There is absolutely nothing wrong with my body." His gaze swept over her appreciatively and she blushed. "That's not what I meant," she muttered.

He parked the car outside the restaurant and within a few minutes they were being seated in a booth. "I already know what I want," Meri said when the waitress brought their menus. "I'd like a chili dog with extra onions and an order of onion rings. And what flavor milk shakes do you have?"

Chet shook his head at her when the waitress brought their food. He'd ordered a chicken salad sandwich on whole wheat and a bowl of vegetable soup. Meri's hot dog was swimming in chili and piled high with chopped onions. Her onion rings were fried to a golden brown and she dipped them in ketchup and tabasco. "You should be arrested for eating that," Chet said, shuddering.

She took a big bite of her chili dog and sighed her contentment. "Are you sure you won't have some?" she asked, and when he shook his head, she gave him an innocent shrug. "I guess this means I'm safe tonight."

"Huh?"

"I doubt there'll be much kissing in the backseat of your car once I swallow all these onions."

Chet frowned. He took his spoon and scooped up a glob of chili and onions. "You're going to pay for this, Meri," he said, then shoved the spoon into his mouth.

*   *   *

Meri clutched the metal railing tightly and watched the other skaters glide across the expansive wood floor. Chet was among them, moving gracefully in time with the song that blared from the giant speakers. His hands were folded behind him, his chin high, as though he didn't have a care in the world. Meri, who assumed he was showing off, had spent the past few minutes praying he would fall, as she inched her way around the skating rink by way of the rail. Thankfully she wasn't the only one hanging on to the rail. There were at least a half dozen others, she noticed, but they all looked to be first- or second-graders.

"Meri, are you going to stand there by the wall all night?" Chet asked, swishing by her. He made a swift turn and dug the toe of his skates into the floor and came to an abrupt halt. Meri frowned. She'd kill herself if she attempted such a stunt.

"You know I don't like heights," she said.

"You're only three inches off the ground."

"Well, it feels a lot higher than that. And I don't remember the first thing about skating."

"You're never going to be able to learn if you don't let go of that rail and get out there and do it."

"Forget it."

He laughed. "Meri, would you just take my hand and let me lead you? l won't let you fall."

"No."

"Aw, come one, Meri."

She looked at him. "You promise you won't let me fall?"

"Swear to it."

She placed her hand tentatively in his. "Now, don't go fast," she warned.

"We're not going to go anywhere until you let go of the rail with your other hand."

"Oh." She closed her eyes and let go. "I'm going to break my neck."

"No, you're not. He chucked softly, firmly squeezing her hand. "Okay, now put your left foot out first and give a gentle shove with your right. Meri, would you open your eyes, for Pete's sake? I don't know one single person who has ever died roller skating."

She opened her eyes. "Now I wish I would have gone to the drive-in. Either way, my poor body is in trouble."

He wasn't listening. "Okay, now. One foot in front of the other. Push off with the opposite foot. That's right, slide forward."

Meri did as she was told, scooting across the floor with baby steps. After a few minutes she looked up at Chet with a tentative smile. "How am I doing?"

"Great," he said, patting her back. "Just remember, when you slide your foot forward, move that side of your body forward as well. It'll help you balance."

After circling the rink several times, Meri was beginning to feel more confident. "You can let go of my hand now, Chet," she said. "I think I've got it." She continued skating, trying to pick up her speed.

"You look like you were born with those things on," he said, grinning at her.

She made several more laps around the rink, picking up speed, gliding smoothly across the floor as though it were glass. Her skirt swirled around her knees gracefully, and her pageboy billowed in the breeze. The wood floor was a blur beneath her skates.

Meri spotted the group of teenage boys about the same time Chet shouted his warning. They were racing, moving in the opposite direction of everybody else, heading straight for her. That was against the rules, she thought, and froze as one of them, the size of a football player, slammed into her. That was her last coherent thought.

The impact was the same as if she'd been hit by a

freight train. Her head was thrown back as her feet left the floor, and she seemed to soar through the air before she fell back onto the floor with a heavy thud. Skaters behind her began to fall like dominoes lined up in a row. Moans and groans reverberated as elbows and knees and skulls collided.

Meri cried out, tears filling her eyes. When she opened them, her vision was blurred and the stars danced before her. She tried to raise her head, but it wasn't worth the pain, so she sunk back onto the floor.

Chet was the first to reach her. He got down on his knees and pulled her into his arms. "Meri, are you all right?" he asked breathlessly, cradling her against his broad chest. "Honey, can you hear me?"

Her eyes fluttered open and she looked into his face. She had to blink several times to see him clearly. "I think I'm okay," she finally answered, and saw his enormous sigh of relief. His cologne filled her nostrils and his roughened cheek grazed her forehead when he pulled her closer. A whistle was blown and Meri saw that the teenage boys had been ordered off the floor. All around her people were beginning to pull themselves up from the floor like weary soldiers. Some were helped by onlookers.

"Do you think you can stand?" Chet asked gently. "Here, let me help you."

With Chet's help Meri managed to pull herself up into a standing position. "I don't think anything is broken," she said, giving him a wry smile, "but I'll probably be sore for a while."

She suddenly realized everybody was staring at her. She smiled as she skated slowly to the edge of the floor and stepped off it, embarrassed when several people clapped as though she were an injured football player coming off the field.

Chet helped her into a chair and knelt beside her to untie the laces of her skates. "I think you've had enough skating for one night, kiddo," he said, smiling tenderly.

"Just tell me one thing," she said later when he dropped her off at her car. "Was I graceful? When I fell, I mean."

He raised one bushy eyebrow. "Do you want the truth?" He shook his head. "No. When you fell, you turned one very clumsy somersault, tripping everybody within ten feet of you. Of course your skirt flew over your head and—"

"Don't tell me any more," she said, covering her face.

"I'm just telling you the truth, honey. Like any friend would do."

"A *real* friend would have lied."

He laughed and gave her a quick kiss. "Don't worry. I still love you."

His words bounced around in her head as she followed him home. She didn't have to check her reflection in the rearview mirror to know she was wearing a broad smile.

Eight

Meri could hear Chet's electric sanding machine before she opened the front door. She found him on his knees in the living room, sanding away dirt and wax and old varnish from the wood floor. She called to him several times before he heard her, and when he did, the smile on his face took her breath away. "Hi, bruiser," he said. "How come you're late?"

Glancing around to make sure they were alone, Meri hurried over to him to receive the kiss she'd been waiting for all day. He wrapped his arms around her and pulled her close, kissing her soundly on the mouth. When he raised his head, she slid her tongue across her bottom lip and tasted the kiss once more. His gaze followed the gesture.

"I stopped by the hospital," she said in answer to his question. She slipped an arm around his waist, loving the feel of him. "I bought the baby a gift and decided to drop it off on the way home." She looked around, surprised the house was so quiet. "Where are Aggie and Bette?"

He smiled. "Gone."

"Oh?"

He pressed his lips against her forehead. "Yeah, you just missed them. They're going to stop by the hospital to visit Stella, then go to dinner and a movie." His smile widened. "A double feature."

"But Aggie hates the movies."

He shrugged. "I guess she changed her mind."

Meri placed her hand against his chest and pushed away from him, trying to keep a straight face. "Did you have something to do with this?"

"Who me?" he asked in wide-eyed innocence.

"Had you any idea they were planning it?"

"Well, they might have mentioned it. Yes, come to think of it, they did mention something about it earlier."

"And?"

His brow wrinkled as if he was trying to remember. "I think I might have told them it was a good idea."

"And?" she repeated a bit louder, trying to suppress a smile.

"I offered to pay their way."

"Ah-ha!" She waved a finger at him. "You bribed them!"

"I think we should try to make the best of it."

"What did you have in mind?"

He grinned, tightening his grip on her so that she was pressed against his lean body. "Dinner at my place."

"That depends," she said, trying to ignore her quickening pulse, "on who's doing the cooking."

"I've already taken care of it."

"Why doesn't that surprise me?"

"I'm just a predictable guy, I guess."

"About as predictable as a Kansas tornado."

He slid his arms down her back to her derriere and smoothed over it with open palms. "How's your bottom?"

"Bruised and sore. Just like my knees." He rubbed

her hips with slow circular motions that made her flesh tingle. "Poor baby," he said, dropping a kiss on her lips. He moved to an earlobe and nipped it gently. She shivered. "Well?" he asked. "What's your answer?"

With her eyes closed she relaxed against him, inhaling the masculine scent of perspiration and cologne. His breath was warm as it fanned her cheek and neck. "I forgot the question."

He chuckled softly. "We were talking about dinner."

"Do I have time to take a shower?" If he kept this up, she was going to need a very *cold* shower.

He nodded. "If you promise to hurry." He raised one brow. "I need a shower too. We could always shower together."

She opened her eyes. "Nice try, but no thanks."

"One never knows until one tries, right?"

He left her at her bedroom door, then continued on up the short flight of stairs to his apartment. "Fifteen minutes," he said over his shoulder. "Don't be late."

Meri hurried into her bedroom, kicking off her low heels and unbuttoning her blouse. She went into the bathroom and turned the water on, letting it warm up while she peeled off her clothes. She stepped under the warm spray and began to think of Chet. Chet as he looked in the morning, clean and fresh from his shower; as he looked when he held her, his eyes burning into hers; as he'd looked the night before, so frightened and concerned when she got hurt. She had at least a dozen images of him in her mind, including the way he'd looked when he confessed his feelings for her. Her heart still beat erratically when she thought about it. She'd been thinking about it all day. When had their relationship begin to change?

Meri emerged from her shower ten minutes later feeling cool and refreshed. In her bedroom she opened her closet and hastily flipped through her clothes. She pulled out a strapless terry-cloth caftan of the same emerald color as her eyes and stepped into it. The elastic band at the top fitted snugly just over her round breasts. In her rush she'd completely forgotten to put on her underwear, and the thought made her smiled wickedly. Wouldn't Chet flip if she arrived without panties? She shook her head. Now, what on earth had possessed her to think such a thing? She was clearly not the seductress type. She located a pair of lacy bikini underwear in her dresser drawer and slipped them on. Next, she stepped into a pair of slingback sandals and raced into the bathroom to run a brush through her hair and dab a drop of perfume behind each ear. A swish of blush over her cheeks and she was ready. Ready for what? she mused, and giggled in spite of herself. Good grief, she was beginning to act like Bette these days.

She climbed the stairs to Chet's apartment slowly, determined to calm the sudden anxiety that had announced itself in the heavy thudding of her heart. She tapped lightly on his door, but it was a full minute before she heard Chet's movement on the other side. When he finally pulled the door open she gasped in surprise. Chet was half naked with only a short, uncomfortably small towel wrapped around his middle. She gaped at him, even as her gaze thoroughly explored his chest.

"Somebody used up all the hot water," he said calmly. "I'm waiting for it to warm up."

"Oh." She was reminded of fine leather as she stared at the tanned body before her. He was lean and rugged and slightly muscular, without an ounce of flab. His upper chest was covered by dark brown curls that grew sparse as they approached his flat stomach. From there they tapered into a slight V-shape and, growing a bit darker, ran down the length of him to where his— She gulped. Well, to where his towel began.

"As you can see," he continued, amusement

lurking in his eyes, "I'm not dressed yet." He seemed to be pleased that she was staring so blatantly at him, and a warm flush suffused her body.

"Er, do you want me to come back?" she managed to ask.

"Don't be silly." He reached for her hand and pulled her into the room. "You're perfectly safe here . . . unless, of course, my towel falls off. Just teasing," he added when she looked as though she were about to run out of the room. "There's a bottle of Perrier in the kitchen. Why don't you pour us each a glass?" He grinned. "Unless you'd prefer something stronger."

"No," she blurted out. "Perrier is fine." Somehow she got into the kitchen without falling on her face, despite the fact that her knees were shaking. What did she need a drink for when she was already stammering and stumbling like she'd been on a binge? She poured the Perrier into two glasses and carried one of the drinks into the living room.

Tossing her head in an attempt to clear her thoughts, she looked around the living room. For the first time since her arrival, she noticed the changes that had taken place in the apartment. They were nothing short of dramatic.

The walls, which had once been faded and washed out, a cross between moss green and cobweb gray, had been painted a cream color. A worsted wool area rug of rust and charcoal on a bone background dominated the wood floor, adding warmth and giving the room a homey feeling. She recognized the old couch that had been in the house when she bought it, the same one Aggie had designated as "needs burning." It now boasted a new slipcover with a high ruffled skirt that blended well with the rug. A solid oak coffee table stood between the sofa and two Scandinavian sling-back chairs, which added a masculine touch to the room. On the other side of the room, against one wall, was an antique drop-leaf table with an assortment of papers lying on it. A brass lamp sat in the center. Meri smiled at the cozy, homelike surroundings. It seemed as though Chet Ambrose was planning to stay for a while.

She took another look at the kitchen and noticed it had undergone changes as well, the most apparent being the removal of Aggie's cooking gear. Aggie had insisted on the changes shortly after Chet had moved in, having spent the past five years of her life complaining about "those damned stairs." So after his ankle had healed, Chet had spent the entire day carrying down no less than six dozen gallon-size cans, along with the massive pots and pans and cooking utensils. He'd built a wall shelf in the main kitchen on which to store them all.

"Like it?" he asked from behind her.

She spun around, surprised to find him already showered and dressed. Well, not quite dressed, she noticed. His shirt was hanging open and he was wearing socks but no shoes. "I love it," she said as he buttoned his shirt. She felt her heart slam to her throat as he unzipped his jeans and tucked the shirt in. Her gaze followed the movement as he slid the zipper back up with his long fingers and fastened his pants. "How did you find time to do all this on top of everything else?" she asked.

"I do it at night." He gave her a crooked smile. "I've . . . uh, needed to work off some of my . . . extra energy."

"Oh." She had half a mind to tell him cold showers were just as effective.

"Why don't you carry your drink into the kitchen?" he suggested. "You can talk to me while I finish dinner."

"What can I do to help?"

"Everything is about ready. You can set the table if you like." He opened one of the cabinets and pulled out two stonewear plates and salad bowls, then handed them to her.

"What smells so good?" she asked.

"Pot roast. With lots of veggies for you." He grinned. "It's one of the few things I can cook without burning to cinders." He opened the refrigerator and pulled out a bowl containing a green salad. "The silverware is in the drawer by the sink," he added as she set the plates and bowls on the table.

"I wish you hadn't gone to so much trouble with dinner," she said. "I don't know how you found time to cook with all you're doing downstairs."

He grinned and pointed to a crock pot on the counter. "I just cut up everything and throw it in the pot, add water and a package of seasoning mix, and *voilà.* Pretty impressive, huh?" He flashed his Groucho Marx eyebrows.

She laughed. "I'm impressed."

"There are some cloth napkins in the drawer below," he said, carrying the salad and a large bottle of Italian dressing to the table.

"You're going all out tonight, are you?" she teased, locating the napkins. She finished setting the table and waited.

He spooned the roast and vegetables onto a platter and carried it to the table. He set the platter down and hurried around to Meri's side of the table, making a big production of seating her, as though she were dining in a plush restaurant. "Your napkin, madam." He took her napkin, flapped it open, and laid it across her lap.

After he served them, they were both silent, concentrating on their food.

"Everything tastes good," Meri said after a few minutes.

"Thanks," Chet said. "How's the new mother doing?"

"Fine. The baby weighed in at almost ten pounds."

"No wonder she was having trouble getting around."

"Would you like to go with me tomorrow to visit her?"

"No thanks. You know I'm not crazy about hospitals."

"Then I hope you never get sick."

"If I do, I'll let you take care of me."

"I'm too busy. Aggie will have to take care of you."

"Then I'll probably learn to like hospitals." He grinned.

Thirty minutes later Meri leaned back in her chair and moaned, turning down Chet's offer of butter pecan ice cream. "I couldn't possibly eat another bite after all that." She patted her stomach. "Dinner was excellent," she proclaimed, "as was the company."

He nodded. "I thought so too." He stood to clear their plates away and ordered her not to move when she started to rise. "You're off tonight," he said.

"The least I can do is carry my dishes to the kitchen."

"No. You're supposed to be recuperating from a skating accident, remember?" He waited until she had reclaimed her chair before he carried the dirty dishes to the sink. "I don't like the way you've been pushing yourself lately," he went on. "What about those girls you interviewed?"

"I hired two of them this morning. They start tomorrow."

"Good. Then you can take the day off."

"Chet!" Her mouth fell open in surprise. "You know I can't do that. Who would train them?"

"Why does it always have to be you?"

"Because there's nobody else to do it. And because it's my business."

"You need an assistant."

She nodded. "I know. I was planning to talk to Stella's husband about taking Aggie's place, but then the baby came and I figured he'd have enough to do for the next few weeks just helping Stella." She sighed heavily, not wanting to get into a discussion about her job right now. She just wanted to relax and forget about everything else for the time being. Chet must have read the look on her face, because he changed the subject.

"Why don't you go into the living room and spread out on the couch and wait for me?" he suggested with a smile.

"Spread out?" she repeated, raising one brow. But she was smiling back at him.

"And I'll bring coffee just as soon as it's finished."

She walked into the living room and lowered herself gracefully onto the couch, kicking her sandals off. She tucked a throw pillow under her head and closed her eyes, listening to the sounds coming from the kitchen as Chet cleaned up. She smiled, feeling comfortably cozy on the big sofa. Her stomach was full, and a full stomach always made her sleepy. She yawned.

Someone or something was nibbling at her ear. She shivered and tried to brush it away, but it reappeared at the base of her throat. Her eyes fluttered open and she looked up into Chet's smiling face. "Darn!" he said. "Why did you have to wake up? I was about to have my way with you."

She sat up quickly. "Did I fall asleep?" she asked, embarrassed. "I'm sorry. You must think I'm a real exciting date."

He sat next to her and pulled her into his arms. "I think you're a wonderful date," he said, tucking her head beneath his chin. "The coffee is ready," he added, pointing to the two cups on the coffee table. She nodded but didn't move, content to let him hold her. When he slid a finger beneath her chin and lifted her face to his for a kiss, she was prepared, knowing she had been waiting for him to do just that. Before either of them knew it, they were locked in a warm embrace, mouths clinging together hungrily. Chet's lips were warm and firm and demanding. He broke away and trailed kisses down her neck and back up again.

"You always feel so good, Meri," he said, his voice a husky whisper.

She never wanted to leave his arms. His hands were painstakingly gentle as he touched her. His fingers feathered across her bare shoulders and her flesh tingled. He pulled her onto his lap and she leaned her head against his shoulder, feeling warm and protected. His cologne was subtle yet alluring. His hands slid down her back, coming to a halt at the base of her spine. He locked his fingers together as though to support her and began moving his thumbs in tiny circles against the small of her back, massaging her, helping her relax.

She melted against him, her energy seeping out of her body. Lethargy swept over her, and her eyelids grew heavy. His circling caresses widened, encompassing her shoulder blades, and she could almost see the hypnotic motion in her mind, pulling her deeper and deeper into a seductive, trancelike state. His fingers traced along her backbone, kneading away tension and fatigue.

His lips captured hers once more with a hunger that surprised her as much as it delighted her. His tongue sought out the warmth of her mouth, and, as the kiss deepened, he lowered her gently onto the couch. He lay on top of her, fitting her soft body against his, and she could feel the heavy pounding of his heart against her breast. He ran one hand down her back to her round hip and massaged it gently, using extreme care with her sore muscles. Heat radiated from his body, and although she was burning from the intensity of it, she could not seem to get close enough. She snuggled deeper into his embrace.

He moaned and pressed his body against hers, and she could feel his hardness at her thigh.

He pulled away slightly and looked deeply into her eyes. "If you want me to stop, just say the word."

She wrapped her arms around his neck and brought his lips back to hers. A tenderness welled up inside of her because of his concern. One word, she knew, would put a halt to his lovemaking, but it was a word she had no use for anymore. She wanted him as badly as he wanted her. "Please love me, Chet," she whispered against his parted lips. He did not hesitate. Still looking into her eyes, he slid off the couch, and pulled her up on her knees for a tender kiss. Then, without warning, he lifted her high in his arms and carried her into the bedroom.

The room was dim, its only light spilling from the partially open bathroom door, casting a beam of golden light across the bed. Through a blur of emotions Meri saw that a change had taken place in this room as well as in the others, and she was reminded of Chet's impeccable taste. But it was not his decorating abilities that interested her at the moment. They could have been in a cave for all she cared.

He carefully put her down on the bed, as though she were made of the most fragile crystal. He kissed her again and again, and when he raised his head to look at her, she thought his eyes seemed to smolder. He moved his hands to the elastic band above her breasts and slowly pulled the material down with trembling fingers. He sucked in his breath as he gazed at her breasts, which in the dusky light looked like white porcelain. He placed his palms over them gently, as if his rough hands might somehow mar their beauty. "Look at you," he said, his tone almost reverent. "Look how beautiful you are. You take my breath away."

She gazed up at him with love-filled eyes. She felt

beautiful. Just looking into his eyes was proof enough. His hands felt wonderfully warm on her skin, like supple leather. She held her breath as he lowered his head and pressed his lips against one rose-crested breast. She placed her hands on either side of his head and held him against her, feeling the most tender of aches inside, a sudden protectiveness that made her want to care for him, defend him if necessary. But the sting of tears behind her eyelids reminded her that she'd been too long without the love of a man. Why had she not noticed it before, this yearning for love? Had her life been too busy? Too reckless?

Chet teased the bud with his tongue in quick strokes, and it hardened and quivered in response. His mouth moved once more to her lips, while his free hand traced the delicate curves of her body. Tiny tremors danced across her bare skin. His tongue teased her lips open, slipping past the barrier of teeth as it sought out the sweetness within. Mouths clung together hungrily, tongues sampled each other. Meri felt her dress slide to her waist and she raised her hips slightly so Chet could pull the garment past her thighs, knees, and finally her ankles. His eyes were bright as he stared at her, his gaze lingering on the filmy panties that clung to her hips and shone iridescent in the room. He pressed his lips against one thigh, then rained kisses down to her knee.

"What are you going?" she asked breathlessly.

He smiled, and his teeth were a brilliant white in the dark room. "I'm kissing your bruises." He stood and unbuttoned his shirt, and Meri noticed how his fingers trembled and wondered if he was nervous or impatient. He tossed the shirt to the floor, and a minute later his jeans followed. His gaze never left her face as he undressed.

She let her own gaze travel his sinewy length, and she almost gasped in appreciation. His cotton briefs hugged his hips and barely contained his arousal. When he pulled them off, exposing his desire, she looked away, flushing hotly. For the first time since she'd entered his apartment, she wondered if she was doing the right thing. Doubt and fear nagged her. It had been so long, so very long.

Chet must have read the uncertainty on her face. He joined her once more on the bed and pulled her into his arms. "I swear I won't hurt you," he whispered. "Please trust me."

She looked into his eyes. She'd come this far, she thought. There was no backing out now. She *did* trust him. She would trust him with her life if he asked. "How can I not trust you," she said, "when I love you so."

His eyes were luminous with emotion. "I love you, Meri," he said, his lips almost on hers. He kissed her. Again and again. His mouth and tongue played havoc with her senses until she was squirming in his arms, her smooth legs grazing his hair-rough ones. His lips skimmed over her breasts and stomach, dipped inside her navel, nipped her thigh, then soothed it with a kiss. She arched her hips, straining against him, her mind pleading for an end to the delicious torture. When he parted her thighs with a knee, she held her breath for what was to come. He entered her slowly, tentatively, and she was swallowed up in a sea of passion. When he'd gained full entry, he waited, as though allowing her body to relax and accept him. His kisses fell on her face and eyelids like summer rain.

She was awash with emotions. She felt fragile and lovely, like a fragrant rosebud coming to life, opening herself, yielding to a brand new dew-kissed morning. Chet's name came to her lips over and over like a sweet song. He answered with a crescendo of kisses. Nevertheless, his body remained perfectly still as he waited for her to initiate the next step in the sensual dance. When she did, he prodded her on, encouraged her, and his words sounded like liquid velvet in her ears. They moved together fluidly, their bodies perfectly attuned, synchronized, as though they'd spent a lifetime practicing together. They fit together perfectly, like two ancient puzzle pieces, his lean rugged lines complementing her curves and peaks.

Meri cried out softly. Desire shot through her body like mercury, splitting her consciousness, and she began to move to a rhythm of her own. Chet's breathing was music to her ears, and she closed her eyes, wanting to memorize the tune forever. She was ablaze, and passion licked its way through every fiber of her being. She sailed over the edge of reality and shuddered in absolute delight. Chet's own movements quickened and he called her name. Together they spiraled into a universe of their own and completed the final steps of their dance.

Time passed. The clock on the bedside table ticked away the minutes, and the only other sound in the room was their rapid breathing as they coasted back to reality. Meri lay curled in Chet's arms, feeling happy and exhausted and more alive than she'd ever felt in her life. Something had let go inside of her. A lock had opened around her emotions, and all the joy and love she'd stored up over the years came flooding out. She loved him! She cuddled against him, pressing against his hard body, seeking his warmth like a kitten who had just come in from the cold.

He hiked up on one elbow and gazed lovingly into her face. "I love you," he said, and kissed her tenderly on the lips. "I've been wanting to make love to you since the first time I saw you. You're not sorry we did, are you?"

"No." She put her arms around his neck and pulled him to her for another kiss. When he raised his head, he was grinning.

"Wait right here," he said, climbing out of bed,

unabashed in his nakedness. He hurried out of the room.

She smiled, wondering what he could be up to. She snuggled down farther under the sheet, taking Chet's pillow with her, hugging it tightly against herself, inhaling his lingering scent. Then she propped the pillow behind her head and gazed around the room absently, noting the changes that had taken place since he'd moved in. Were the changes he'd made in her as obvious as those in the apartment? She smiled softly. She *had* changed. She felt more lovely and feminine, and more in love than ever before. She closed her eyes and saw his face as he'd looked when they'd made love. She wanted to lock that memory in her mind forever.

"I thought it was the guy who always fell asleep afterward," Chet said from the doorway, rousing Meri from her daydreaming. Carrying a hefty bowl of butter pecan ice cream, he slid into bed beside her. Tucked cozily in the warm nest of his bed, they shared the ice cream, licking their spoons like greedy children.

They talked, sharing common interests and feelings. Meri laughed at Chet's stories and shared with him her fears and inadequacies, things she'd never told anyone in her life. He listened, squeezing her hand at intervals. Later, he surprised her with a few insecurities of his own.

"I used to think I had to have a lot of money to be happy, to be somebody," he said, clasping his hands behind his head and staring up at the water-stained ceiling tiles. "I thought success meant living in the most exclusive section of town, or eating at the best restaurants, or wearing the most expensive clothes."

Meri listened, hanging on to every word, wanting to find out more about the man she loved. She wanted to know his insides like she knew her own. "And did it?" she asked.

"No."

She snuggled closer. "So you decided to give all your money away and move into this dump."

He looked pained. "This is *not* a dump," he said emphatically. "When I get finished with this place, it's going to look like a palace."

"Okay, okay," she said, laughing. "I believe you."

"And no, I did not give my money away." He grinned. "I'm not stupid, you know. Let's just say I've learned it takes more than money or success to make a person happy."

He pulled the covers away from her body and stared at her hungrily. He ran his fingers over her flat stomach in a featherlike caress that caused her to suck in her breath sharply. "What do you plan to do with your life now?" she asked, trying to pick up the thread of their conversation.

"Now?" he said, leaning over one perfectly rounded breast. His tongue flicked lightly against the pink nipple, and it instantly hardened. He raised his head a fraction, one brow cocked in an amused look. "You mean this instant?"

She nodded, watching him stroke the other nipple with his index finger. It quivered under his touch. "Instead of telling you what I plan to do right now," he said, letting his hand glide down her inner thigh, "why don't you let me show you?"

But for Meri, who had spent the better part of her life in submissiveness, first under her father, then her husband, Chet's suggestion was not entirely acceptable. "I believe you've already shown me," she answered coyly. "Now, why don't you lie back and let me show you?"

"Know what I think?" Aggie asked waspishly the next morning, glaring across the breakfast table at Chet and Meri.

Meri sipped her coffee, then tore her gaze away from Chet's smiling face and looked into Aggie's scowling one. "Huh?"

"I think if you two keep grinning at each other like that, you're going to have to have your ears relocated to the tops of your heads."

"What's that?" Chet asked in a disinterested voice, glancing at Aggie for the first time that morning. "I didn't hear you."

Aggie crossed her plump arms over her breasts. "I was just saying how thankful I am that my grand-daughter isn't here to watch you two make love to each other at the breakfast table."

"Aggie!" Meri felt her cheeks burn.

"Are we that obvious, Aggie?" Chet asked, his eyes twinkling. He winked at Meri.

Aggie leaned forward on both elbows. "I just hope you know what you're doing," she warned him, ignoring Meri's protests, "and nobody gets hurt."

The smile faded from Chet's face. He reached over and patted Aggie's hand. "Don't worry," he said, his tone sincere. "I have no intention of letting anybody get hurt."

Aggie settled back in her chair as though appeased by his words. She looked from one to the other. "Guess this means we'll be having those steps repaired out back," she said, matter-of-factly, "now that you two will be wanting to slip upstairs and do heaven-knows-what to each other." She rolled her eyes toward the ceiling. "It's absolutely wicked the way you two are looking at each other," she said. "Especially over breakfast. Absolutely wicked!"

Nine

Meri tried to concentrate on the grocery list she was preparing for a client, but her eyelids kept drooping, reminding her she'd lost another night's sleep. After two weeks of sharing most of her evenings, as well as some of the early mornings, with Chet, it came as no surprise she was exhausted. She merely wondered how she would continue to do so and still operate a demanding business. Somehow, she knew she would. Even if it killed her. She took another swallow of bitter black coffee and shuddered. The coffee would probably kill her first. Unfortunately she was finding it difficult to live without the caffeine-enriched brew, which probably accounted for the bouts of insomnia she suffered long after she returned to her own empty bed each night.

She gazed out the window at the half-empty parking lot that surrounded the condominium, watching the heat bounce off the black asphalt in shimmering waves. It was Saturday. Anybody with half a brain would be at the lake, she thought, seeking solace from the unbearable temperatures. September had settled in and still the weather refused to cool. Every day there were record-breaking highs in the nineties. It was sheer misery. Aggie seemed the hardest hit by the heat, becoming more obstinate and irritable than anyone would have thought possible. She suffered headaches that forced her to bed long before the sun finally disappeared below the horizon. Meri was beginning to worry about her and promised herself she would speak to Stella's husband about taking over the cooking. But with Stella still on maternity leave, Herb was forced to work double time at his cousin's catering service, so Meri didn't know when she'd have the opportunity to speak with him. With training the new girls, there just wasn't time. She sighed, rolling her head from side to side to loosen the tight muscles. When had life become so hectic?

The telephone rang. When she answered it she recognized the husky baritone voice instantly. "Have I told you lately how crazy I am about you?" Chet asked.

She thrilled to the sound of his voice, her lips curving into a smile. That was how she felt about him too. Crazy. And soft and happy and very feminine. "Not in the last hour and fifteen minutes," she answered, glancing down at her wristwatch.

There was a throaty chuckle from his end. "Are you insinuating that I call too often?"

"It just amazes me how you can always locate me. I'm in and out so much." She dropped into a nearby chair and kicked one leg over the side. She closed her eyes and could see his face as he must look right now. As he'd looked the night before. It made her warm and tingly all over.

"Aggie's book," he said. "She's got a duplicate of yours, remember? I just keep dialing numbers until I find you."

"Which explains why neither of us gets anything done," she said, trying to keep the humor out of her voice. She kicked off her shoes and tucked one foot beneath her, letting her head fall back against the chair. "Have you finished painting my bedroom yet?"

Another soft chuckle. "No, but I had a wonderful time touring your underwear drawer. I came up with several pairs of sexy undies."

She gasped, bolting straight in her chair. "Chet, you didn't!"

"It was an accident," he said. "The drawer fell out when I tried to move the dresser away from the wall. Your . . . er, unmentionables flew out all over the floor."

"So you naturally decided to look at each item."

"I think your bedroom is going to be a problem," he confessed, his tone amused. "Every time I try to get something done in there, I start thinking about you lying soft and warm in that bed, and I get all—"

"Never mind about that!" she interrrupted, unable to shake her discomfort at having Chet handle her underthings. "You've been working on that room for a week now," she admonished him, "and I'm sick and tired of having to step over paint cans and messy dropcloths.

"Meri?" Her name was spoken in a husky purr.

"What?" She sank back into the chair.

"Do you know what I thought about when I saw them . . . your undies, I mean?"

His gentle voice soothed her frazzled nerves, rocked her with caressing tones and vibrations. She surrendered, her insides becoming warm and fluttery. "No, what did you think about?"

"I thought about how beautiful you look when I make love to you," he answered, his voice raspy. "How your lips are so sweet and open to my kisses. I thought about your body, how soft and curved it is, how it molds perfectly to mine. I can't stop thinking about you. I can't stop wanting you."

She shivered. Her toes and fingertips tingled as he

made love to her with his words. "I feel the same way," she said. "It's all I think about anymore."

"I'm glad, honey. That's why I decided to call you." He hesitated for a moment before going on. "I want to spend the weekend with you. There's a place north of town. I know you've heard of it. The Elms? We could drive up there, be there in forty-five minutes."

Meri opened her mouth to speak but nothing came out except a strangled "Oh?"

Chet began to talk quickly. "This place has an indoor spa. We could swim or sit in a Jacuzzi or play tennis, whatever you want. The food is great. We could just lie around and relax and be together. Just you and me."

Her speechlessness ended. "Chet, are you out of your mind?" she asked in disbelief. "I can't just go away, just like that!" She snapped her fingers for emphasis, despite the fact that he couldn't see her. "I can't just walk away from my obligations and spend the weekend at a—a hotel." She lowered her voice on the last word.

"Yes, you can."

"W-with a man," she went on. "Have you forgotten I have a sixteen-year-old daughter, for goodness' sake? I can't very well flaunt an affair in her face."

"This is not just an affair. I happen to be deeply in love with you."

"I mean, what would she think if I just went running off to a hotel with a man? Good grief!" She ran out of oxygen and was forced to take a breather.

"She would probably be happy for us," he said. "But I happen to know that Bette is spending the weekend with what's-her-name at the lake."

"LaDonna?" Meri had forgotten about that.

"Uh-huh."

"What about Aggie?"

"She'd welcome the chance to get rid of us. Spend the weekend with me, honey," he said imploringly.

"I can't, Chet. I've got to make up the schedule and buy food. . . . What with Stella still on maternity leave and those new girls who don't know the difference between a dustmop and a toilet brush . . ." She sighed heavily. "I just can't. That's final."

"Can you be ready in two hours?"

"Make it three."

Merideth Anne Kincaid, the same woman who'd almost thrown up from sheer nervousness on her honeymoon, the same woman who'd insisted on making love in the dark during her entire married life, was going to a hotel with a man. Not just any man, mind you. She'd known this one less than eight weeks. Meri slid down lower in the front seat of Chet's car.

"Meri, would you take off those gaudy sunglasses?" Chet asked. "You look like a punk rock musician."

She glanced over at him. "I already told you, they belong to Bette. They're all I could find."

He laughed. "Well, next time you want to travel incognito, don't wear hot-pink sunglasses. People will stare."

It was after six o'clock when they pulled into the parking lot of the rustic Elms Resort Hotel. Although the sun was still high, the temperature had dropped, taking the airless humidity with it. The Elms was located in the older section of a tiny Missouri town called Excelsior Springs. The area was best known for its mineral water, which was believed to have a healing effect on some ailments. The original Elms, Chet told Meri, sounding like a tour guide, was built in 1888 to house those tourists who came to "take the waters." It burned, as did the one built after it. The third and present structure was completed in 1912, constructed of limestone and concrete in the hopes it would not suffer the same fate as its predecessors.

Meri thought the hotel looked like something from an Agatha Christie novel. Perched on a hill, the massive stone building loomed overhead against a backdrop of blue sky. Its exterior was completely lined with wrought-iron fire escapes. "This looks like a great place for a murder," she said as Chet helped her out of the car. Nevertheless, she was awed by it.

He grinned, studying the building himself. Then he leaned past Meri and grabbed their bags from the backseat. "But why should I want to murder you, sweetheart?" he asked, giving a terrible Bogart impression. "I've got other plans for your lovely little body."

She cleared her throat discreetly. "How do you plan to register us into this hotel?" she couldn't help asking.

"I've already taken care of everything . . . in my name," he answered casually, closing the car door with a single thrust of his hip.

"Do you think they'll believe it? I mean, that we're actually . . . er, man and wife?" She glanced warily in the direction of the entrance.

Chet laughed and stared pointedly at the crisp muslin skirt and jacket she was wearing. Her starched blouse with its scalloped Peter Pan collar was buttoned to her chin. "People don't worry about stuff like that anymore," he said, and chuckled again. "Anyway, you hardly give the impression of recklessness."

"What's that supposed to mean?" she asked, scrutinizing her attire self-consciously.

"Nothing is wrong," he said quickly. "You look beautiful as always. Just unbutton your top button. You look like you're ready to receive your first communion."

"It doesn't look right . . . I mean, with this particular outfit."

"Aw, come on, Meri. Loosen up!" he teased. He set

the bags down and unbuttoned the button. "There. Now you look brazen as heck."

She gave him an icy stare and stalked to the hotel entrance. As he opened the door for her, she edged away from him in haughty silence.

"Yeah, that's it, honey," he said. "Now we look married."

Once inside the lobby Meri was instantly overcome with a feeling of elegance and grace. It was like a scene from a late-night movie, she thought, and half-expected to see Fred Astaire and Ginger Rogers dance by at any moment. One wall was completely dominated by a monstrous stone fireplace, over which hung an antique tapestry that had become worn and tattered over the years. The furniture was dark, ornately scrolled, and marbled.

If anybody at the reception desk suspected their relationship, Meri couldn't see it in their courteous and professional smiles. Why couldn't she just relax and enjoy herself? she wondered. Because she was thirty-five years old and had never done anything like this in her life, she answered herself.

The bell captain led them to an elevator. "Is this your first time?" he asked, grinning over his shoulder at Meri.

She stiffened, her hand automatically reaching for the button on her blouse. She buttoned it. "I—I beg your pardon?"

Chet chuckled softly. "I think he wants to know if this is your first visit to the hotel." There was a mischievous twinkle in his eye.

Meri shook her head as the elevator door clanged open. "No. But I've . . . I mean, we . . . my . . . er, husband and I have heard great things about it." She fidgeted with her clothes as they stepped into the elevator. The doors floundered closed and they were jerked upward to the next floor.

"This way, please," the bell captain announced as

they stepped out into the hall. He walked ahead, glancing over his shoulder once to make sure they were following.

The hallway yawned before them. Miniature lights in frosted glass shades hung from polished brass chains along the walls and lighted their way. The hall was carpeted in an old-fashioned print that was worn along the center, where traffic was heaviest. Meri was warmed to her toes by the scene. It evoked feelings of pleasure, like coming in from the cold and finding a roaring fire in the hearth. Like freshly baked chocolate-chip cookies. Like rainy Sunday afternoons. She felt Chet's gaze on her and knew he was waiting for a reaction. She smiled. "You've really got a thing for old places," she whispered. "This reminds me of home."

He took her hand loosely in his own. "Did you know it's for sale?"

"Really?"

The bell captain came to a halt in front of a door and slipped a key into the lock. "This is one of our larger rooms, Mr. Ambrose," he said, pushing the door open. "You'll have a view of the pool area."

"I'm sure we'll like it," Chet answered, allowing Meri to enter first.

She took in her surroundings while Chet discussed various aspects of the hotel with the bell captain. The room was large, the ceilings high. A marble vanity stretched across one wall in the bathroom, over which hung a large mirror with beveled edges. She heard the door close and turned around. Chet was watching her expectantly.

"What do you think?" he finally asked.

"I think it's wonderful," she said, nodding her approval. She saw his eyes light up and knew her opinion was very important to him for some reason. "But it needs work." She gave the room a final, unsparing scrutiny. "Fresh paint and new carpet for one thing. And I would toss out the drapes and bed-spread and buy new ones."

"I agree."

"It would certainly present a challenge. But the place has character. And that elevator . . . It seems to have a—a personality of its own."

"I was thinking the same thing."

"Why?" She raised both brows. He had that look on his face, the same look he'd had when discussing his plans for renovating her house. It excited her.

"Why what?" he asked.

"Why are you thinking about it? I mean, why are you so interested?"

He shrugged. "I was just thinking what it would look like fixed up. It could be a showplace. It would attract people from all over the world." He sat down on the bed. "Of course, it would cost a fortune . . . a couple of million to buy it and another million to fix it up."

"Yes, but who has that kind of money to invest?" she asked indifferently, dropping onto the bed beside him. She crossed her legs and swung one back and forth as she continued to study the room. She could see it just as she felt Chet would, with fresh paint, new carpeting, new drapes and bedspread.

"I could probably arrange the financing," he said absently, gazing at her shapely leg.

She looked at him in surprise. "Chet, you don't have that kind of money." She continued to watch him. "Do you?"

He shrugged. "I've stashed away some over the years and made some good investments." He refused to meet her eyes. "I got a pretty good profit from the stores I've already sold. Plus, it looks like I'll have my two stores in Kansas and Missouri sold within a matter of weeks."

"But three million dollars!" It may as well have been a billion. She gave him her full attention now.

"I could probably save a quarter of a million by contracting the work out myself. I'm just not sure I want the headaches involved in such an operation." He frowned. "Think of the paperwork."

"Is this why you brought me here?" she asked, giving him a suspicious look. "So you could show me this place?"

Her question seemed to amuse him. "Not entirely," he answered, his gaze sweeping over her appreciatively. "I've already seen the place a couple of times." He grinned devilishly as he reached for her, pulling her easily onto his lap. "I'll show you why I brought you here," he said huskily, his fingers working at the tiny buttons on her blouse.

She didn't resist him as he slid the garment down her arms. Her head fell back in absolute surrender as he nuzzled his face at the hollow of her throat and pressed warm kisses along one collarbone. She laced her fingers through the curls on his head, loving the silken texture of the dark hair. Still cradling her in his arms, he captured her lips in a warm and tender kiss. As the kiss deepened, he leaned back on the bed, taking her with him. They lay side by side, and their eyes met and locked, speaking of love. Meanwhile, their hands were busy touching and fondling and evoking pleasure.

"Do you know what it's like being with you and not being able to take you in my arms?" he asked softly, stroking her hair. "Every time I look at you I feel like Aggie is going to pounce on me. She's very protective of you, you know."

Meri smiled. "She's always been like that. She's not as forbidding as she looks."

He sighed. "I know. But I don't like having to hide my feelings or slip around to be with you. I want to tell the whole world how I feel about you." He kissed her. "That's why I wanted to bring you here," he said, cupping her face with his palms. "So I could touch you and kiss you whenever I liked. So I could look at you the way I want, without Aggie reading my mind. You do so many things to me, Meri. So many wonderful things . . ." He let his voice trail away as he kissed her again and again. He took her hand in his and kissed her palm, then lowered her hand slowly, pressing it firmly against his slacks, where his hardness proved his growing excitement. "See what you do to me, Meri?" he whispered against her parted lips. She felt her pulse quicken as she gently caressed him, loving him for being so wonderfully masculine.

He removed the rest of her clothes slowly, kissing each inch of her flesh he bared. His mouth was warm, his breath heated, as his lips glided across the silken valley between her soft breasts. Eagerly Meri unfastened his shirt buttons, and in minutes his clothing was deposited on the floor beside hers.

Lying naked in each other's arms, they made love slowly and with painstaking thoroughness. Meri pressed her body against his, running her hands along the rippling tendons that stretched across his back. She trailed her fingers over his shoulders and plunged them into the mat of curls that covered his chest. His nipples were warm and nubby as she flicked them lightly with her tongue, and she watched in fascination as they hardened like her own did when excited.

"You're so adorable . . . and sexy," Chet said, and covered her mouth once more with his. He pressed her flat across the bed and took a pink nipple between his lips, toying with it until it quivered. She crooned with pleasure as he continued to suckle at her breasts. Yet she was growing impatient, too, no longer able to ignore the heat cascading through her entire body. She shifted restlessly on the bed. As though reading her thoughts, he found the sensitive area between her thighs and delighted in bringing

her to full arousal. She arched against him, pleading
with him to take her. She didn't have to ask twice.

As always, Chet's entry into her body unleashed
such intense feelings of pleasure, Meri thought she
would surely die from it. His eyes, as he looked into
hers, told her he felt much the same. She curled her
arms around his neck and brought his mouth to
hers. He began to move slowly against her, whisper-
ing words of love, raining soft kisses over her face.
She closed her eyes and gave in to the wonderful sen-
sations. Her thoughts were filled with Chet. She loved
him; she worshiped him. She clung to him breathlessly, her fingers splayed at the small of his back. Her
body was hot, sensitized to his slightest touch. The
sheet whispered against her head as she moved it
from side to side in delicious agony. A fire burned at
the very core of her femininity. It grew and grew until
it burst into a feeling of such incredible delight that
she cried out, blinking back sudden tears of release.
"I love you," she said over and over again until her
words sounded like a chant.

Chet's eyes were liquid with love and desire. "And I
love you," he said before losing himself in her softness. She felt him sink against her in complete aban-
donment, heard him whisper her name once before
he shuddered in her arms.

She wanted to lie there forever and inhale the scent
of him. It was heady and intoxicating. Exhilarating.
She smoothed her hand over his chest and stomach,
where a light sheen of perspiration had appeared as
unobtrusively as morning dew. His breathing was
still labored and his heartbeat rapid. She closed her
eyes and listened, loving the sounds of his body. His
stomach growled once and she smiled. When his
breathing returned to normal, he tightened his arms
around her.

"I think it's only fair to warn you, Meri," he said as
though thinking out loud. "I've reached a point of no

return with you. I knew it was going to happen, but I was powerless to stop it."

She wasn't sure what he was trying to tell her. "What do you mean?"

He gazed down at her lovingly. "I'll never be able to let you go now." He smiled almost apologetically. "I'm afraid you're stuck with me."

The laughter that bubbled up from her throat was spontaneous. She felt as light and free as a cloud. "Good," she said in a satisfied voice, "because I was just about to tell you the same thing."

They lay for several minutes in silence, each content to merely hold the other close. "You know what I'd like to do," Chet said, propping himself up on one elbow. "Something we've never done before—"

She laughed softly. "At this point in our relationship, I can't imagine what that could be."

"Take a shower together," he said with the eagerness of a young boy. "We've never taken a shower together. Come on." He slid off the bed and captured her hands in his. When she pulled the sheet up higher over her breasts, he grinned. "Come on, Meri. No time to be shy. I've already seen every gorgeous inch of your body." He leaned over, scooped her up in his arms, and carried her to the bathroom, despite her objections.

Meri found herself laughing in spite of her sudden shyness. "You're crazy, do you know that?" she said as he set her down on the tiled floor.

"Crazy in love with you," he answered. "Now, don't move. I'm going to turn the water on." He slid open the shower door and turned both handles until, with the clanging of hidden pipes, water sputtered from the nozzle. He adjusted the temperature and stepped inside the shower. "Come on in, the water's fine."

She joined him tentatively and heard him slide the shower door closed. He took the bar of soap from the soapdish and unwrapped it. "Here," he said, handing it to her. "Wash me."

She glanced up quickly and saw the challenge in his eyes. She sucked in her breath. Why was it so much easier to touch his body when she was dazed with passion? she wondered. Now, with him standing before her with water dripping from his hard body, she felt bashful. She was not used to these intimacies. Martin had clearly defined the boundary lines early in their marriage. He was a stickler for locked bathroom doors. Washing one's body was a chore, not something done for pleasure. Had he ever summoned her into the shower to do what Chet was now requesting, she would have fainted dead on the spot. She swallowed. Her hands were trembling slightly as she held the soap under the steady stream of water. She turned to Chet and pressed the bar against his broad chest and began rubbing him in circular motions. With the help of his chest hair she was able to work up a thick lather. She could sense his gaze on her face as she moved her hands down his hard stomach.

"Okay," she chirped, trying to keep her voice steady. "Turn around."

He chuckled softly, but did as he was told. It was obvious she had purposely avoided washing all of him. She began soaping his back, watching the lather stream down to his firm buttocks. Chet Ambrose was a beautiful specimen of a man—lean, hard, and tanned. "All finished," she announced.

He turned around slowly. There was an amused glint in his blue eyes as he cocked his head to the side. "You missed a spot," he said, but didn't press her. Instead, he took the soap from her and worked up a rich lather. Then he spread the foamy mixture across her breasts and stomach and thighs. He turned her around and repeated the process on her back and hips, sliding his hands along her graceful curves. "You're blushing," he said, slapping her play-fully on her derriere. She spun around and he cap-tured her slippery body in his arms and kissed her, cupping her soft hips in the palms of his hands. The kiss deepened.

Meri pulled back first. "We're going to be late for dinner," she said, gasping for air.

Chet grinned. "You're probably right. But some things are worth being late."

When they entered the dining room sometime later, Meri felt as though she'd just taken a trip into the past. An ornate wood-paneled bar dominated one wall. Behind it, beveled mirrors reflected the lights from a brilliant chandelier that hung in the center of the room. A beautifully gowned woman played on a grand piano at one corner. The soft music flowed across the room and blended nicely with the steady hum of chatter and the clinking of crystal. On the far side of the room a waiter ignited a dish, and the blue flame rose high into the air, capturing the attention of those dining nearby. Meri could barely eat her din-ner for staring both at the room and at Chet.

Chet signed the bill after they had demolished their steaks. "Ever been in a hot tub?" he asked Meri, never looking away from her parted red lips as he spoke.

"No, but I'm willing to try anything at least once," she answered, a teasing glint in her eyes. Her stom-ach was full, her body relaxed and satisfied after their lovemaking. Love and happiness radiated from her, as they did from the man sitting across from her. Nothing else mattered at the moment, not her job nor her responsibilities, nor Aggie and Bette for that mat-ter. Only Chet.

He took her hand in his. "You're like a different per-son tonight, Meri. You needed to get away. Haven't you ever just picked up and gone away for the weekend?"

She dropped her gaze. "Martin never liked to go away," she said. "He blamed it on his job. He traveled a lot. By the time the weekend rolled around, all he wanted to do was lie on the couch and watch television. I guess I couldn't blame him."

"And there hasn't been anybody else?" he asked, smiling. It was obvious he already knew the answer.

Meri straightened in her chair. "As much as I'd like to give the impression of easygoing sophistication, the answer is no."

He squeezed her hand. His eyes bore into hers, sharing with her a very private look, one that told her more than he was able to voice out loud at the moment. "I really don't have any right to say this," he began, "but I'm glad. I want to be the one to show you how wonderful things can be between two people who really love each other." He almost whispered the next statement. "It's not often two people find what we've found together."

She nodded. How well she knew. His words touched the core of her heart as he gazed at her in a way that made her stomach flutter. She had never felt this way and knew without a doubt no other man would affect her as deeply as Chet did.

He stood up and walked around the table to her in a lazy, leisurely manner. But when he leaned over her and spoke, his voice was husky with desire. "Let's get out of here before I rip that dress off you."

She rose from the table, objectively scrutinizing her attire. The dress, which was strapless and clung to her breasts and stomach, was the best and most provocative one she owned. From the waist it fell in soft folds that swirled at her knees when she walked. "Don't you like it?" she asked as they left the dining room.

Chet ushered her out of the restaurant. "Yes, but

your nipples have been pouting at me all evening. It's about to drive me out of my mind." His gaze was glued to her soft breasts as he spoke. He swallowed. "Besides, you and I have a date with a hot tub."

The New Leaf Spa reminded Meri of an underground city. They entered it by way of a long concrete tunnel, where warm steam prevailed and clung to the walls. Clad in bathing suits, they passed several mineral baths and the beautiful and exotic European swimming pool that were tucked beneath the hotel. Chet led Meri to a reception desk, where they were given oversize towels. They were shown several "environmental rooms," and Meri selected one called the Oriental Room because it reminded her of a Japanese bath house. In the very center of the room sat a large Jacuzzi that looked hot and inviting.

Chet led her to the tub and she stepped tentatively into the hot water, watching it swirl up around her ankles, her knees, and finally her thighs. Chet lowered himself into the massive tub, and tugged on her hand until she sat beside him. He flipped a switch at his elbow and the jets along the sides of the tub shot into motion, causing the water to bubble and gurgle and massage their flesh.

"What do you think?" he asked, leaning his head against the tiled wall.

She closed her eyes. "I think it's wonderful," she said, giving way to the laziness she was feeling. "But I don't think I'm going to be able to stay awake much longer."

Back in their hotel room, they curled up in bed together just as the late movie started, an old Bette Davis film. But tucked in the crook of Chet's arm, Meri found it difficult to follow the plot of the story. Her eyes were blinking furiously, and she finally succumbed to the drowsy feeling that washed over her.

*   *   *

Meri felt something trying to wake her. She resisted. The bed creaked. She sensed movement. Something moist and delightful teased the back of her neck and forced her sleepy brain to attention. A husky chuckle sounded at her ear. Chet. "What's going on?" she asked, rubbing her sleep-filled eyes.

He pulled her into his arms and kissed her, stroking her blond hair. "Do you realize this is the first time we've ever woken up together?" he asked.

She yawned and stretched. "What about the time I fell asleep in your apartment?"

He laughed. "That doesn't count. You were in such a tizzy trying to get back to your room before Bette or Aggie woke up. But I'll never forget the look on your face." He kissed her again. "Are you happy?" he finally asked, his blue eyes gazing searchingly at her.

"Hmmm. More than happy."

He raised himself up on one elbow and she was entranced by how the morning light bathed his face in gold. "Tell me again how much you love me," he said. "I want to hear it over and over again."

"I do love you, Chet," she whispered, her eyes sparkling with love.

"Is it good between us?" he asked.

She sensed the questions that lurked behind those blue eyes and loved him all the more for it. He wanted comparisons. But then, he was only human. How could she answer truthfully without being unfair to Martin's memory? "Chet, I've never known anything like what we have," she answered honestly. "I've never been so completely loved and treasured by anyone in my life. And I've never loved a man in return like I love you."

He kissed her tenderly, one hand at the small of her back, pressing her close against his lean body. He lifted her head and grinned. "Does that mean you'll agree to take showers with me-whenever I ask?"

"Yes. Whenever it's possible," she added, knowing he would understand her meaning.

He dropped the smile and his eyes grew serious. "Meri—" He hesitated only a second. "Do you love me enough to marry me?"

She felt her heart somersault, landing somewhere in the back of her throat, making it difficult to swallow. "Yes," she answered at last, touching his cheek with her fingertips. "I love you *more* than enough to marry you."

"Okay, so when's the wedding?" Chet asked.

"Huh?" Meri glanced over her shoulder for one final look at the Elms Hotel as they drove away. She hadn't wanted to leave.

"When are we going to get married?" He didn't wait for her to answer. "I think we should do it as soon as possible. How about tomorrow?"

"Tomorrow!" she shrieked. "We can't get married tomorrow!"

"Why not?"

"Why not?" she echoed in disbelief. "Because, I—" She paused, fighting the urge to laugh out loud. The mere idea was ludicrous. "Because I have to meet my cleaning girls first thing in the morning, that's why."

"Then we can get married in the afternoon," he said simply.

"No, Chet," she said, holding both hands up to stop him. "I've already told you I need time." She saw his jaw harden and tried to smooth over her words. "You want me to be able to concentrate all my efforts on being your wife, don't you?" she said softly. "The least you can do is wait until I get my business affairs in order."

"How long?" His words were clipped.

She took a deep breath. "Six or eight weeks."

He scowled. "I'll give you two."

"Are you crazy? I need at least six weeks, Chet."

"You know how much I want this, Meri. I'm tired of sneaking around in order to be with you. But I'm willing to meet you halfway. I'll wait a month. Exactly one month from today."

"Okay, one month," she agreed, desperately hoping she'd be able to get everything squared away at work. Of course, it would be a simple wedding, nothing fancy. She'd have to pick up a new dress, check into getting a marriage license, call one of the judges to marry them. Hopefully she would have the girls trained by then and Stella would be back. Unless there were complications. She pressed her fingers to her temples and sighed. All her problems had seemed so far away during the last twenty-four hours. Almost nonexistent. Now she realized she'd only put them on hold.

"So when are we going to tell them?" Chet asked.

"Tell who what?" she murmured absently, wondering when she was going to have the opportunity to talk to Herb about coming to work for her as a cook.

"When are we going to tell Aggie and Bette we're getting married?"

Meri wasn't really listening. "Let me think on it for a while."

He looked surprised. "Don't you plan to tell them right away?"

"I don't know, Chet. With Aggie in such a vile mood these days, I'm afraid to say anything to her."

"Do you think she'll be happy for us? She doesn't really like me, does she?"

"Who, Aggie? Of course she likes you."

"She does?" he asked in surprise. "How can you tell?"

"Well . . ." She paused. "She hasn't thrown you out of the house yet. That's always a good sign."

"What about Bette? How do you think Bette feels about me?"

"Bette is crazy about you." She patted his leg affectionately. "Stop worrying."

"Do you think I'll make a good father for her? What do you think she should call me?"

Meri laughed. "How about Chet? That's a good name."

"We'll throw a big party so I can meet her friends. I think it's important to know all her friends, don't you? To sort of open the lines of communication."

"I hope you know what you're getting yourself into," she said, laughing.

"We can take family vacations together," he continued. "We'll drop Aggie off at one hotel and we'll stay in another."

She laughed. "You're terrible."

"Just kidding," he said, giving her a wink. "And I'll have to meet your parents. Do you think they'll like me? Did they like Martin? What are they like?"

"Chet!" She covered her ears. "How do you expect me to answer all these questions?"

"I think we should tell everybody right away," he said decisively. "Surprise them. I can't wait to see the look on Aggie's face."

"Chet, I think you'd better let me tell Aggie in my own way," Meri said, reaching for his free hand. She squeezed it reassuringly. "I expect she'll be happy for us, but I want to wait until the time is right before I tell her, when she's in a better mood."

They looked at each other. Then suddenly they were laughing. "That could take days," Chet said.

It did.

Ten

"There is absolutely no way we can get everything ready for a wedding in just three weeks!" Aggie announced the following weekend, shortly after she and Bette had been given the news. Bette had been ecstatic and on the telephone ever since, passing the information on to her friends. Meri's mother had cried when Meri had called long distance to give her the news, insisting that she bring Chet up as soon as possible for the family to meet him. Now Aggie was standing in the middle of Meri's bedroom, ticking reasons off on her plump fingers why the wedding couldn't be held in three weeks.

"First, you need a caterer. You've *got* to let someone else take care of the food. Then there's the flowers . . . and the invitations . . . and the license. . . . And you'll have to find somebody to marry you. And what are you planning to get married in, for Pete's sake, your pajamas?" She heaved an enormous sigh of disgust. "You're not even listening to me!"

Meri slathered the ivory-coated paintbrush along the baseboard and frowned. Excess paint ran down the wood and onto the moss-green carpet. "Darn!" she muttered, grabbing for a roll of paper towels. Chet had made it look so easy. "I'm listening," she said to her mother-in-law, wishing now she'd kept her mouth shut about her plans to marry Chet. What had started out as a simple wedding in front of a judge now threatened to rival Princess Diana's. But she'd barely managed to keep it a secret this past week. Her insides had been so filled with the knowledge and expectancy until she thought she'd burst if she didn't tell someone. She pressed the paper towel to the carpet, letting the paint bleed into it. "Chet and I want a small wedding," she said for the umpteenth time. "Just family." Paint was running all over the carpet now. Where the heck was Chet anyway? "The only way I'll agree to have it at home is if you promise not to invite more than twenty people."

"Which brings us to another problem," Aggie continued. "Look at this place. We'll never have time to finish it."

Meri squinched her eyes closed and pressed her fingertips to her temples. "Do we really have to discuss this right now, Aggie?" she asked. "I've got a splitting headache. On top of that, the paint is all runny and—" She halted. "Where is Chet?"

"How should I know?"

She sighed heavily and leaned back, palms pressed to the floor behind her. "If you must know, I'm going to ask Stella's husband, Herb, to prepare whatever food we need. So you can stop worrying about it."

"What about the cake?"

"I'll think about the cake later." Meri began picking up the paint litter and stuffing it into a garbage bag. "Didn't Chet tell you where he was going?"

Aggie shook her head, still frowning at the names she'd written down for the guest list. "All he said was he'd be back in an hour. That was two hours ago."

"Well, he's going to have to finish painting this

room," Meri declared, rising from her crouched position. "I've got a million things to do."

"If it was my wedding, I'd want to take my time and do it right," Aggie said. "After all, you're like my own daughter. The least you could do is let me give you a nice wedding. I'll pay for it."

Meri smiled at the woman, warmed by her generosity. "Aggie, I appreciate it. But Chet and I don't want anything big and fancy. We want this wedding to be quick and simple."

"You're not pregnant, are you?"

"Aggie!" Meri's mouth fell open. "Of course I'm not pregnant!"

"Then what's your hurry? You two already do everything married people do."

A splash of crimson appeared on Meri's cheeks. "We are *not* sleeping together . . . now. We decided to hold off until after the wedding so we wouldn't have to slip around." She couldn't help but wonder how she and Chet were going to last that long. It was getting difficult to be in the same room together. "Not that it's any of your business," she added. "You know, I was hoping you'd be happy for me."

"I am happy. Thrilled to death. But I don't want to get stuck with all the work."

"You're not getting stuck with all the work. I am. But I can't do everything this second, you know. Good grief! We only decided to get married last weekend."

"You mean you knew all this week and didn't say anything to me?" Aggie demanded, her voice rising.

"After today it should be obvious why I kept my mouth shut about it."

Aggie crossed her plump arms. "All I'm saying is we need more time. That's the problem with you, Merideth Anne. You don't take time for anything. You live your life going ninety miles an hour and expect everyone else to keep up with you." She eyed her daughter-in-law suspiciously. "And who is going to take care of the business while you're away?"

"Away?" Meri arched one brow. "Where am I going?"

"Well, heavenly days, girl! You mean you haven't even decided where you're going for your honeymoon?"

Meri bent down and pressed the lid back onto the paint can. "I doubt we'll even take a honeymoon," she said, "unless we just go away for the weekend or something. We'll have to wait until I get caught up."

"Have you bothered to tell Chet?"

"Tell Chet what?"

They both turned and saw him standing in the doorway. Meri melted a little when she saw his grin, then sighed.

"Where have you been?" she asked. "I thought you were going to help me paint this room."

"I had something very important to take care of," he answered, tiptoeing into the room, trying not to step on the paint-splotched newspapers that lined the floor.

"Meri and I were just discussing your honeymoon," Aggie said, giving Meri a defiant look. "Or should I say lack of."

"Speaking of honeymoons," Chet said, smiling rakishly at Meri. He reached into his back pocket and drew out an envelope, handing it to her.

"What's this?" she asked.

"It's our honeymoon," he announced proudly. "You don't think I'd let my wife miss out on the most important thing, do you?" He didn't wait for her to answer. "I just wasn't sure I could arrange things in time, the last minute and all." He reached over and opened the flap for her. "It's two tickets for the SS *Scandinavian.*"

"Huh?" Her mouth dropped open.

"For the day after we're married," he said, hugging her. "Surprised?"

"I think dumbfounded is a better word," Aggie said, giving her daughter-in-law a knowing look.

"It's a two-week Caribbean cruise, honey." He laughed. "Look at her, Aggie. She's speechless."

"Yeah," Aggie mumbled. "Well, I think I'll mosey on out of here before she mutters those first words. You two let me know if the wedding is still on after today . . . before I go out and spend a fortune on something to wear." She closed the door behind her.

Chet's blue eyes filled with anxiety. He released Meri and dropped his arms to his sides. "What's that supposed to mean, if the wedding is still on? You're not having second thoughts, are you?"

"Of course not," she said in a choked voice.

His relief was obvious. "Well, don't scare me like that. Look inside, honey," he said, indicating the envelope. "There's another surprise in there . . . my wedding gift to you."

Her heart hammering against her ribs, she pulled out the contents. Five crisp bills stared at her. "Five thousand dollars?" She stared at him in disbelief.

"For shopping," he said easily. "You'll need to buy all that stuff women are supposed to buy for their honeymoons. You know, see-through nighties, lacy undies—important things." A wicked gleam filled his eye. "And the rest is to cover wedding expenses. You can have whatever kind of wedding you want, simple or elaborate. I know we'd decided on small, but just in case you change your mind. And you let me know if that's not enough."

Her eyes filled with tears, and a single drop fell on her cheek. "Chet—" She stopped and tried to get her voice under control. "I never . . . never expected all this."

He took her in his arms. "I know you didn't, honey. You've got too much class for that." He pulled back and wiped away the tear with a finger. "But I'm not going to let you go into hock over this wedding. I'm paying for everything." He smiled. "That's what I'm here for, to take care of you. You no longer have to be afraid to be alone or have to worry about finances. I'm going to take care of everything from now on. I've already paid for our honeymoon in full."

"But you should have told me," she said, her voice quavering. "Before you actually spent the money."

He shrugged. "I didn't know for sure if I'd be able to swing it, to book passage, that is. The boat was full. We got in on a cancellation. And it's a suite on the top deck. Supposed to be very nice. Anyway . . ." He gave her a tender look. "I wanted to surprise you. I want everything to be perfect for you," he said, his voice husky with emotion. "And I was afraid you'd object to the cost, you being so prudent and all." He grinned. "I can tell I'm going to be the only frivolous member in the family."

Her heart went out to him. She glanced down at the money and tickets. "I appreciate the thought, Chet," she said, and gulped back the lump in her throat. "But I just don't see how I can . . . how we can go right now. Stella won't be able to come back to work for at least two more weeks, and I can't just run off and leave her and Aggie with everything."

"Surely you can take two weeks off, Meri," he said, giving her a gentle pat on the rump. "For vacation. Even the crummiest jobs in the world come with a two-week vacation. Besides, you don't even need that job now that we're getting married."

She looked at him, startled. "Chet, I never said I wanted to quit my job."

"I know you didn't. But I can see how wound up it keeps you. I can support you now. You don't have to put up with all that nonsense . . . or those men. They don't need you half as badly as I do. You can quit today if you like." He smiled proudly. "Tell you what. You could even come to work for me if you want, if I decide to buy that hotel. You like to paint, don't you?"

"I detest it," she said, giving him a cool stare. "Any-how, why should I want to quit my job . . . excuse me, my business, when I've worked so hard to build it? It's been my whole life these past five years."

"That's right, it *has* been your whole life, your *only* life. Now I'm a part of that life and you don't need it."

She clenched the envelope in her hand. "Are you trying to tell me what I do or don't need?" she asked crisply.

He frowned. "No. But I am going to tell you what *I* don't need. I don't need a wife who spends all day run-ning around like a crazy lady and comes home exhausted and irritable."

"But I'm not sure I'm ready—or willing—to give it up."

"What are you trying to say?" His words were clipped.

"I'm saying that you should have talked to me before you just assumed I'd give it up."

He let out a colorful expletive. "Then don't give it up. But don't expect me to sit around waiting for you to get home just so you can fall asleep in my arms."

"Well, for your information, I've been managing fine for the past five years. My health is perfect and I haven't collapsed or even been sick for that matter."

"Yeah, you've been managing just fine," he said sar-castically. "That's why this place is falling down around you, why you and Aggie chew each other's heads off constantly."

She gave him an indignant look. "I certainly haven't noticed you breaking your neck lately to get this place in shape," she said, her green eyes snap-ping. "It's taken you two weeks just to tear this one room apart. Heaven only knows when you'll get around to painting it! Every time I go to bed I drag wet newspapers in with me. Just look at this place!"

His face hardened. A muscle ticked in his jaw. "I've

been tied up with business. I do have other interests, you know."

"No matter how fleeting."

He ignored that. "I'm surprised you've even had time to notice this place," he said. "You certainly don't take time to notice anything else around here. Like your own family, for instance. Especially your daughter."

"What's *that* supposed to mean?"

"Only that you don't have time for her. When's the last time you've done anything for her or taken her anywhere? Other than to work," he added quickly. "Have you forgotten about Bette? She needs you, too, you know. No wonder she's boy-crazy. She's just looking for a little affection. Like the rest of us," he mumbled.

Meri was speechless, her eyes wide in horror. "You don't know what you're talking about," she said, her tone as cold as freshly fallen snow.

"Bette stays at the lake most of the time, because it's the only home she has. While, ironically enough, her mother is out trying to make homes for every bum in town."

"That's a lie!" Tears streamed down her face. "I've given Bette a good home . . . the very best I could!" A sob rose in the back of her throat and escaped in a heartrendering moan. "How dare you criticize me, you who have everything! At least I make an honest effort at working!"

"Oh, so we're going to harp on that subject again, huh?"

She swiped angrily at the tears. "I'm sorry if the subject of your laziness bothers you."

One side of his mouth curled a smile, but the look in his eyes was anything but happy. "Laziness?" he drawled, as if the word were foreign to him.

"You criticize me for what I do, but look at you," she said. "You just sit back and let your employees do everything, let them build your little empire. Then, when you grow bored with it, you just sell out. You don't care about responsibility or obligation. You don't finish anything. Look!" She waved her hand around the room. "You can't even finish painting one stupid room." She flopped down on the bed, letting the tears fall, tears of anger and frustration and fatigue.

Chet had stood very still during the tirade, his eyes dark and forbidding. Now those eyes held an expression of pain and his shoulders sagged in defeat. He shuffled through the strewn newspapers to a chair and fell into it. After a moment of silence he began to laugh, but the sound was not of gaiety, but of sorrow. "You're right, Meri," he said. "I guess I don't seem very responsible to you, do I?"

Hands trembling, Meri reached for a roll of paper towels and peeled off a sheet. "It doesn't matter," she said, dabbing her eyes. She felt weary, her energy drained from the argument. "It really doesn't."

"But that doesn't mean I don't know anything about hard work," he continued, as though he hadn't heard her. "I've done little else for the past twenty years." He slumped back into the chair and clasped his hands together until the knuckles were white. "I know what it's like to be successful, Meri. It used to be the most important thing in my life." His expression was mournful. "To me, working was the same as breathing. I look back on that time now and don't understand why it was so important, only that it was."

"We don't have to go into this now," she said, seeing the painful emotions playing across his face.

"Yes, we do." He stood and jammed his hands into his pockets as he started to pace the floor. "A couple of years ago I had to make some decisions in my life." He let his eyes meet hers for a moment. "You wouldn't have recognized me then. I weighed a lot more than I do now. I drank and smoked too much." He ignored the surprised look on her face. "Work had become such a habit for me that I had replaced everything in my life with it. I had nobody, no family, no one in particular who gave a damn about me except a few women who enjoyed what my money could buy. In return they gave me emptiness. Empty emotions. Empty sex."

He sighed heavily. "Then I got sick. I began bleeding my guts out. I figured it was cancer or something like that, so I didn't bother going to the doctor until it was too painful to live with. I thought I was dying and that scared the hell out of me. For the first time in my life I realized I had never actually begun to live. I thought I'd lost the one chance I had." He took a deep breath and sat back down. "I finally went to the doctor and found out I had ulcers. Several of them, one of them as big as my fist." He held up a fist and studied it for a moment as though he still found it hard to believe. "Part of my problem was stress, I'm sure. All I thought about was work, improving sales, building bigger stores, topping last year's quota. I had headaches no amount of pills or booze would stop. But I just kept right on drinking and popping pills and hoping they would go away. The doctor told me I'd be dead in a year if I didn't change the way I was living."

Meri hadn't realized she was crying. Silent sobs racked her body until she was breathless. "What did you do?" she asked, trying to swallow fresh tears.

Chet raised his own tearful eyes to her, eyes that were so vulnerable in pain. "I chose to live." He stared at her for a long time and the silence in the room hung like a thick fog. "I changed my life dramatically just by selling some of the stores. I gave up smoking and laid off booze. I started taking care of myself. I decided living was the most important thing in the world to me." He paused. "It still is."

It was several minutes before Meri could speak, and

when she did, her words were choked and her voice unsteady. "Please believe me when I tell you that I love you," she began, her heart wrenched with emotion. "More than I've ever loved anybody in my life, more than I thought possible." She hesitated, trying to find the right words, trying to make him understand. "But I need something else in my life. I love you, but I'm not going to live in your shadow. I'm not going to live in anyone's shadow. I'm not going to let another person tell me what to do or what to say or how to feel. No matter how much I love that person." She brushed away more tears. "Because no matter how much you come to love or depend on someone, you still have to be able to count on number one, count on yourself. Can't you understand any of this? My job has given me back all the things I'd lost when I was married to Martin. Self-esteem, confidence, independence. I can't give them up now! Not when I've worked so hard to get them."

Silence fell again. Chet seemed to be pondering her words and getting his emotions under control. He tried to speak, but coughed and had to start over again. "There's only one problem with your plans, Meri," he finally said. "There's no room in them for me. I never wanted to run your life. I only wanted to share it with you and to love you. But I don't think I'd be happy spending the rest of my life waiting for you to have time for me." He shrugged and ran one hand through his thick curly hair. "Maybe we've rushed things. Maybe we need to think things over, find out what we really want." He strolled to the bed and picked up the envelope she dropped. "Anyway, I don't think I can just sit by and watch you kill yourself." Another second and he was gone.

More than an hour had passed since Meri heard Chet's car pull out of the driveway, and still she remained glued to her spot on the bed. Surprisingly neither Bette nor Aggie had ventured upstairs, as though respecting her need for privacy and letting her suffer the tears alone. Therefore, when Bette's hysterical screams rang out through the silent house, it jolted Meri right out of her senses. Her heart in her throat, she tore out of the bedroom and almost slammed into her panic-stricken daughter on the stairs.

"It's Aggie!" Bette blurted out. "I—I think she's dead!"

Fear shot through Meri, rendering her immobile for a matter of seconds. She clung to the banister, her mind reeling. "Aggie?" Her brain clicked, releasing adrenaline into her system, and she cleared the remaining steps in record-breaking time. She reached the kitchen door and gasped in horror. Aggie lay before her on the kitchen floor, completely still.

"Oh, Aggie, no!" Her wail was an order, a plea, summoned from the very depths of her soul. She knelt beside the woman, gathering her up in her arms. Attempts to revive her proved fruitless. "Bette—" It was hard to speak; her tongue was plastered to the roof of her mouth. "Call an ambulance!"

Eleven

The width of the hall that led into the emergency room could be measured by ten twelve-inch squares, half white, half black. Lengthwise, there were thirty-two squares. That would mean sixteen black ones and sixteen white ones. Meri had counted and recounted. Of course, it wasn't a fair count because the hall took a sharp right at the reception desk, and that naturally meant there were more squares running down the next hallway. From where she sat, she was not able to count the remaining ones that encompassed the entire emergency room, and she didn't dare leave her chair. She might miss the doctor. Therefore, she'd have to stop counting. Stop the game.

Then what?

How long it had taken her to fill out the necessary forms she couldn't say. But when she had ventured back to the information desk to ask about Aggie, the nurse had simply replied, "They're working on her." Meri had nodded as though that made complete sense to her and she went back to counting squares.

Working on her. How did one work on a human being? she wondered. On flesh and blood. It sounded so impersonal. Did they know who they were working on, how important she was, how much she was loved? Meri felt the tears slide down her cheeks. Once again she stopped a skittering nurse and questioned her, her own voice coming from a tunnel somewhere deep inside.

"Her doctor has arrived," the nurse said hurriedly. "He's checking her now." Meri marveled at the way her white cap bobbed up and down as she talked.

Meri had known this numbness before when Martin died. First the shock. Then pain and emptiness and fear. She blinked. Fear? No, she wasn't really fearful this time. No matter how much she loved Aggie and had come to depend on her, she wasn't afraid of facing life without her. She would go on. Just as she'd gone on without Martin. She almost cried in relief. It was as though a giant stone had been removed from her shoulders. She was no longer afraid!

There was movement. A shadow fell across the floor, distorting the perfect squares. She raised her eyes slowly to his face. More numbness. "How did you know?" she asked.

Chet lowered himself into the chair beside her. "Bette told me. She's waiting by the telephone. Have you heard anything yet?"

"Only that they're working on her." The words still sounded strange. "Her doctor is with her now." *Thank you for coming*, she added silently. *I don't think I can stand sitting here much longer without knowing.* Could he see it all in her eyes?

"Meri?"

"What?" His eyes looked different now, she thought. Somber.

"We . . . You and I need to talk. Not right now. Later." It was a request, spoken softly, compelling her to comply. "I still love you, Meri. No matter what happens, remember that."

She nodded. "The paramedics said something about a stroke." She had to tell him, let him know how things looked for Aggie, for the woman who'd been just like a mother to her for the past five years. "I didn't want to ask them a lot of questions, take up their time." She squeezed her eyes shut, but a tear managed to escape anyhow. "Chet, I think Aggie's had a stroke."

His arms went around her soothingly, transferring the warmth of his body to her own frozen limbs. "We don't know that for sure," he said, his soft voice offering hope and strength. "We don't know how bad it was. Let's not suspect the worst."

More tears. "I—I can't help it." She choked back the sob in her throat. "You know what the worst part is?" she asked, turning her tear-stained face to him. "I can't even remember the last time I told her how much I loved her. And she's done so much for me. She taught me to believe in myself, Chet. I always thought I was weak, but Aggie wouldn't hear of it. She said I had more grit and backbone than most men she knew."

He chuckled. "That's sounds like Aggie, all right."

Meri sniffled. "My mother always taught me that I was supposed to learn how to do for a man. My big goal in life was to marry and raise a slew of kids. I always felt limited. Aggie taught me that I could do anything I damn well pleased. That's the way I want Bette to grow up thinking." She blushed at the mention of her daughter's name. "I love Bette, Chet, do you know that? I never meant to neglect her or make her think she didn't have a home."

He took her hand and lifted it to his lips. "Meri, please forgive me for saying what I did. You're a wonderful mother. I said those things only to hurt you, because I was hurting."

She leaned her head on his shoulder, content to sit in silence for a while. She loved him. Somehow they would work out their problems.

"How long have you been here?" he asked.

"I don't know. A couple of hours, I guess. Seems much longer."

He gave her a funny half smile. "You and I seem to spend a lot of time in hospitals."

She laughed in spite of the tears that continued to trickle down her face. "Who knows? Sooner or later you'll probably grow to like them."

"I doubt that," he muttered.

Time passed. Meri cried some more, salty tears that streamed down her cheeks, leaving her face bloated, her eyes painfully red. Chet paced the floor, offering encouragement, constantly staring at the doors, looking for anyone who might give them some news. They waited, and finally, when Meri thought she could stand no more, she heard her name called. She jumped up from her chair, recognizing immediately the man who'd summoned her. Aggie's doctor.

She was beside him in an instant, grasping his liver-spotted hands, staring anxiously into his eyes. "Dr. Saunders." It was the barest of whispers. "How is she?"

The doctor must have read the terror in her eyes. He squeezed her hand. "Now, calm down," he said. "Aggie is going to be fine." His voice was unnaturally loud, as though to better reach her, to exorcise her worries. "She's suffered a slight stroke, but she's going to be okay." He glanced up at Chet inquiringly.

Meri permitted only the briefest of introductions before she continued her questions. "Is she paralyzed?" she asked, her heart thumping wildly.

"Let's sit down," the doctor suggested, indicating the chairs. He squeezed Meri's hand once more before letting it go. "There's a slight chance of paralysis in her facial muscles," he said. "I'm sure it's only temporary. We'll have to run more tests, of course, but these things have a way of working themselves out. I have every reason to believe that she will recover from it."

"May I see her?" Meri asked, her eyes pleading.

"Why don't we let her rest tonight," he said. "She's heavily sedated right now anyway. She won't even know you're in the room."

"What caused it, Doctor?" Chet asked.

The doctor looked at him, crossing his arms over his chest. "It's simple. She hasn't been taking her medication."

Meri blinked. "What medication?"

"For high blood pressure." He eyed Meri skeptically. "You mean you didn't know she was on medication?" He muttered a curse. "Snippety old bag. I told her what would happen if she didn't keep those prescriptions filled."

Meri shook her head, trying to absorb the information. "How long has she been having problems?"

The doctor scratched his head as though making mental calculations. "I reckon a year, year and a half. I don't have her file with me."

"She never mentioned it. She's always taking something. I asked her once. She told me they were vitamins and hormones. She has been taking a lot of aspirins lately."

"She's been having headaches too," Chet said.

"Been irritable?" the doctor asked.

Chet grinned. "It's hard to tell with Aggie."

Dr. Saunders smiled and nodded. "Like I said. Snippety. She's too ornery to die. Has she been smoking those godawful cigarettes?" he asked Meri.

She shook her head. "Not that I know of. She gave those up a long time ago."

"Well, I reckon she did follow some of my advice then. If she hadn't, I can't rightly say if she would have pulled through this or not."

"How long are you planning to keep her here?" Chet asked.

"Week or two. I'm going to order some tests first thing in the morning, do a brain scan, see how things look." He shrugged. "I don't expect I'll find much damage, she's too darned hardheaded. Anyway, her vital signs look good." He looked directly at Meri. "I think this was just a warning, you see. It's Aggie's body telling her to either slow down her motor or jump ship."

Meri nodded. "Just tell me what I can do, Doctor. I'll do anything to help."

"Stop looking so worried," he answered immediately. "Your mother-in-law is going to have to change her lifestyle if she wants to stay on this earth a while longer." He glanced at his watch and pulled himself up from the chair. "I got to go, and you should go home, too, Meri." He looked at Chet. "You seem to have more sense right now than this young lady. Take her home and make sure she doesn't worry herself into a fit." He shook his finger in her face. "I don't have time to treat both you and Aggie."

Chet nodded, gazing solemnly at Meri. "I'll make sure of it, Doctor."

Meri couldn't sleep. Bette had long since come in to kiss her good night and waited while Meri called the hospital to check on Aggie's condition. Afterward, she and Bette had sat cross-legged on the bed, sharing stories about the woman who had been such a large part of their lives for the past five years, and whom they both loved dearly.

Bette had an uncanny knack for impressions and kept Meri entertained with some of Aggie's fiery dialogues. Amazingly the girl had every action and quirk down to a T.

"Just who do you think you are, Bette Kincaid," the

girl had said, "for wearing thirty-seven pair of underwear this week? The Queen of England?" She had
puckered her lips for a better effect. "And just who do
you think is going to wash them, huh? You'd better
hire yourself a maid, young lady. Yessiree!"

Meri had laughed so hard tears had streamed down
her cheeks. "Stop!" she had pleaded, holding her ach-
ing sides, knowing Bette's mimicry was done in love
for her grandmother. Aggie had almost raised her,
and Bette worshiped the woman. As Meri had
watched her daughter, so slender and graceful, she
had had difficulty keeping herself from swelling with
pride over her own creation. She had felt very close to
Bette, knowing they shared so many feelings. Had
she really alienated her daughter these past couple of
years? she had wondered, desperately hoping she
had not. She would make it up to her, give Bette the
kind of home she deserved. Thank heavens she had a
second chance. Life was so short, almost fleeting.
One had to grasp it and squeeze the moments out.
Tomorrow they could be gone. Aggie's stroke was
proof of that.

Bette had given Meri one final hug, making her
promise to wake her early for the trip to the hospital.
Then, throwing her mother a kiss from the doorway,
she had left the room and closed the door.

Now, more than an hour later, Meri was as wound
up as the sheets that had twisted around her slender
legs from her constant tossing and turning. She was
exhausted, but her mind kept going over the events of
the day, her argument with Chet, the ordeal with
Aggie, the long but fruitful telephone conversation
she'd had with Stella and Herb that evening. It was
enough to give her a case of the screaming meemies.

She sat up and kicked her covers off, then turned
on the lamp on the bedside table. Aimlessly she
flipped through the pages of a magazine, staring at

the print without really seeing it. Finally, she tossed the magazine aside.

If it hadn't been for the absolute silence of the house, she would not have heard the soft knock on her bedroom door. Thinking it must be Bette, she called out her welcome, keeping her place in bed.

Chet peered around the door. "Are you still awake?"

Meri automatically reached for the sheet, pulling it up over her breasts, scarcely covered by her flimsy nightgown. "Yes, come in," she said, wishing she hadn't washed off her makeup.

He closed the door behind him and stood there, his hands in the pockets of his snug-fitting slacks, the same pair he'd worn to the hospital. "If you're tired, I can come back." He avoided eye contact.

"No, please." Her heart thudded loudly in her chest. "Sit down." To her surprise, he didn't take the chair across the room but walked straight to the bed and planted himself at the foot of it. His body was stiff and formal.

"Have you checked on Aggie?" he asked, lifting his gaze hesitantly.

She nodded, not daring to meet his blue eyes. "I called the hospital earlier. It seems Aggie came out from under the sedative while a nurse was checking her vital signs." Meri smiled at the thought. "Aggie told her if she didn't get out and leave her alone she was going to make the rest of her rounds wearing a bedpan."

He laughed. "Recovery is on the way."

"By morning she'll have made enemies of the entire staff," Meri added, fidgeting with the bedcovers, anything to keep her from meeting the look in his eyes. "Something tells me they're going to release her just as soon as they can."

Silence. Then suddenly they were laughing, although it was difficult to say who initiated it. It lifted the strain between them for a moment, so Meri welcomed it. Then Chet clasped his hands in front of him, staring down at his knuckles as though trying to gather his thoughts.

"Meri?" he said, looking up at her. "I think it's time we had a talk." One corner of his mouth curved into a semblance of a smile, easing the seriousness of his tone.

Something fluttered in her stomach. "I was thinking the same thing. I—"

"No, wait." He held up one hand. "Let me go first. I've been thinking about this all evening, but I may not have the nerve to make the offer again."

Confused, she waited, wondering what it could be. "I'm listening."

"It's about your business," he began, positioning himself on the bed so that he was facing her. "I've been thinking that perhaps you could use another hand in it, someone to help you out." He stopped her when she opened her mouth to speak. "Especially now . . . with Aggie sick."

"What would you do?" Meri asked, unable to contain her curiosity.

"Simple. I'd cook." He rushed on. "You know, I *can* cook some things. Maybe not all the exotic dishes Aggie prepares, but I could learn. I'm a fast learner, Meri. I'd even go a step further and make the deliveries for you. Hoping, of course, to give you the freedom to spend more time with me." He smiled proudly. "I've got it all figured out."

"Chet, stop," she said, her heart going out to him. This was, she knew, a supreme sacrifice on his part. Knowing that he loved her enough to make it was the conviction she needed to go ahead with her own plans. "I appreciate your offer," she said, "but I've decided to sell my business."

She may as well have told him she was going to dye her hair green, his look was just as incredulous. "But why would you want to do that?" he asked. "You've worked so hard."

"That's just it. I've always wanted to run a business, Chet, but I never wanted the business to run me. Like this one has."

"I never meant for this to happen," he cut in, as though he still didn't understand her reasoning. "I'd never ask you to sell it."

"I'm not doing it for you," she said. "I'm doing it for me. This isn't the first time I've thought about it. You're right about my needing help. My business needs a team effort. Until this year Aggie and I were doing fine. But the business just grew and grew." She grinned, throwing her hands up in the air. "What can I say? It was a success!" She lowered her hands and smoothed the sheet over her thighs reflectively. "I've often thought how perfect Stella and Herb would be for it. Lately the thought has occurred more often."

"But . . ." He shook his head as though all this were not sinking in properly. "You told me earlier that you needed a job for yourself, so that you would never be afraid to stand on your own two feet."

"I'm not afraid of that anymore, Chet," she said, and smiled. "I haven't crumbled so far, have I? Anyway, I've got another business in mind, one that can be bigger and better. And still leave me time for my family," she added softly.

He covered his face with his hand, but he was grinning. "I should have known," he said dryly, peeking out from between his fingers. "What does the lady tycoon have up her sleeve this time?"

"I'd like to go in with you on this hotel thing."

He dropped his hands and his eyebrows shot up in disbelief. "What? I mean, why?"

She didn't falter. "Because I think it's a sound investment, that's why. And because I think we could make money on it. From what my attorney has already told me—"

"Your attorney? You've already talked to an attorney?"

"I just called him and asked him what he thought about the place. He told me he thought it was a gold mine for anybody who had the money to restore it. He's digging up information on it for me." She gave Chet an indignant look. "You don't think I'd just jump into something before making a thorough investigation, do you?"

"You should have asked me," he said. "I've got tons of information on the place."

"I didn't want to say anything until I was sure it was what I really wanted to do." She lowered her eyes, fingering the covers once more. "I've been thinking about it all week," she confessed, "but I still hadn't made up my mind about it when we . . . er, talked this afternoon. I think I felt pressured, like you were trying to rush me into doing something I wasn't sure about." She looked at him and her eyes were pleading for him to understand. "I wanted it to be my decision."

He shook his head in confusion. But what would you do, Meri? You obviously hate to paint." He grinned. "And we both know you have no flair for decorating."

She shot him an icy look. "There are other areas I think I can handle more than adequately," she said, and began ticking them off on her fingers. "For instance. Somebody has to manage the whole thing, to remind you about deadlines—"

"You mean *hound* me, don't you?" he interrupted, smiling.

"Someone has to push the paperwork," she continued, unperturbed. "You don't want the stress that's involved with running a business, where, I, on the other hand, thrive on it. From what I understand, you're more interested in the construction end of it, making renovations. But once you buy that place, there's going to be a million more things to do. Like hiring and managing personnel, marketing, public relations. Naturally you'll have to keep the place in operation while you're working on it. You don't want to lose your profits." She ignored his look of amazement. "I *could* get involved with some of the decorating." He winced. "However, I would let the final decisions rest with you. Who knows, we may be able to learn something from each other."

"It all sounds good to me," he replied easily.

She waited a second before going on. "There's just one stipulation. I'd prefer we operated as partners."

"Partners?" This seemed to amuse him.

"Now, I don't expect you to hand it over to me, just like that," she rushed on, snapping her fingers for emphasis. "I plan to buy my way into the business."

He crossed his arms, his eyes bright with humor. "How much money are you planning to invest in this . . . er, partnership?"

Meri didn't blink. "Fifty thousand dollars."

"Whoa!" He sat up straight, no longer looking amused. "Where did you get that kind of money?"

"I don't exactly have it right now, this instant," she said, "but I will have it." She refused to meet his eyes. She didn't really want to disclose all the details of her plan.

"I think you'd better give me a little more information on this, Meri," he said, staring hard at her.

She took a deep breath. So he was going to play tough. Okay, she had gone this far. "Part of the money is from Martin's insurance settlement. I was saving it for Bette's education. The other money will come from the sale of the house."

"Wait a minute!" He glanced around the room, a look of disbelief on his face. "You're not actually thinking about selling this place." It was more a statement than a question.

"I have to," she said. "I'm going to put Aggie in one of those retirement condominiums. It's what she wants and I'm going to see that she gets it. Stella and Herb have agreed to buy my business and pay by monthly installments, all of which will be mailed directly to Aggie. I want her to be able to live in complete comfort for the rest of her life." She shrugged. "Anyway, half the money from this house belongs to her. We bought the place together."

"Then I'll buy Aggie's retirement villa," he said, "as my share of the equity in this house. I don't want you to sell this wonderful old house, Meri. And I love Aggie just as much as the rest of you. I'll make sure the old buzzard doesn't want for anything." He crossed his arms. "As for the insurance money, it stays right where it is, for Bette."

"I would need the money only temporarily," Meri argued. "Naturally I'd hope to be able to replace it by the time Bette goes to college."

"You're not doing either," Chet said, his words clipped.

Meri raised her chin defiantly. She was not about to ask this man for a handout. "Why?" she demanded.

"Because I want to continue living in this place after we're married, that's why. And because I don't need your dead husband's money. I'm willing to go along with you on a lot of things, Meri. I want our marriage to be a fifty-fifty relationship. But this is one issue I'm going to stand firm on."

A look of pure astonishment spread over her face. "You mean, you still want to go through with the wedding?"

Suddenly, before she even knew what was happening, Chet had moved the entire length of the bed and pulled her into his arms. "Of course I want to go through with it. Did you think I'd give you up that easily, honey?" His face was only an inch from hers. His breath was warm on her face. "I love you, Meri. I need you." He kissed her hungrily, thoroughly, and the intensity of it left them breathless. When he raised his eyes to hers, they were serious. "Look, I don't want to talk about this money thing again. I'll agree to anything but that."

"Yes, but—"

"No buts." He squeezed her hand. "Listen, lady, I don't want to dominate you or force you to live in my shadow, as you say, but as your husband I will want to protect you and love you and give you what's mine. I've worked hard all my life and made good money doing it. Is it so bad that I'd want to share it with my wife, to make her life a little easier?" Before she could answer he kissed her again. "Is everything agreed on?"

"How can I argue with you?" she asked. "Every time I try to open my mouth, you cover it with yours." Her eyes were bright and love-filled.

"Good." He kissed the tip of her nose as if sealing their agreement. Then, trailing a finger over her soft lips, he gave her a self-satisfied smile. "I want to know just one thing. What changed your mind? About selling your business and coming in with me?" He snuggled closer. "Come on, Meri," he teased. "Feed my ego. Tell me it's because I'm wonderful and irresistible and that I'm a good lover." He lowered his head and pressed his lips against the hollow of her throat.

Her heart skidded to a stop and her flesh tingled all the way down to her toes. "I just took a long look at my life," she said honestly as he looked up at her again. "Having my job made me feel good about myself, assured me that I would always be able to make it on my own." She smiled self-consciously. "I know this all sounds silly to you."

"Not in the least," he said softly, his eyes full of love. "I know how much you've worried about that in the past."

She dropped her gaze. "But I'm not afraid to stand alone anymore. I love you, Chet. More than I've ever loved anybody. And I want to spend the rest of my life with you. But if something were to happen to you, I know I wouldn't crumble. I would be able to pick myself up and go on. Knowing that is very important to me." She saw the proud smile he gave her. "And even though I still want to be involved in a career, I don't ever want anything to take up so much of me that I don't have anything left over for my family. I realize now how important you and my family are. I guess I've rearranged my priorities and settled on a compromise."

"Are you happy with your decision?" he asked. "I mean *really* happy?"

She planted a soft kiss on his mouth. "*Really* happy," she said.

"Oh, Meri." He nipped her earlobe and slipped one hand beneath the sheet to caress her thigh. A husky moan escaped his throat and his hand moved upward.

Meri wriggled against him, finding it difficult to concentrate on anything else except what his hand was doing. "Ahem," she said softly. "I—I thought we'd agreed to . . . er, hold off until after the wedding. So we wouldn't have to slip around anymore."

"We did," he agreed in a raspy voice. "But as long as you're making compromises"—one brow arched up and he grinned devilishly—"I thought you might make one more."

And that's exactly what she did.

THE EDITOR'S CORNER

We've got a "Super Seven" heading your way next month. First you'll get our four romances as always during the first week of the month; then on October 15, we'll have **THE SHAMROCK TRINITY** on the racks for you. With these "Super Seven" romances following up our four great LOVESWEPTs this month and coming on the heels of Sharon and Tom Curtis's remarkable **SUNSHINE AND SHADOW**, we hope we've set up a fantastic fall season of reading pleasure for you.

Leading off next month is **STILL WATERS**, LOVE-SWEPT #163, by Kathleen Creighton who made a stunning LOVESWEPT debut with **DELILAH'S WEAKNESS. STILL WATERS** is a love story that sparkles with whimsy while proving that old saying "still waters run deep." Maddy Gordon works with troubled children, using puppets in play situations to reach them. Wary and self-protective, she also uses her puppets to fend off people who dare to get too close to her. Nothing, though, can keep Zack London away from her. This forceful, sexy, loving man didn't win Olympic Gold Medals by fading when the going got tough, so he isn't about to be deterred by any obstacle Maddie can put in his path. This is a richly emotional love story that we think you'll long remember.

Barbara Boswell's **WHATEVER IT TAKES**, LOVE-SWEPT #164, works a kind of physical magic on a reader—melting her heart while taking her breath away. When feisty Kelly Malloy is teamed up against her will with irresistible hunk Brant Madison to do a story on illegal babyselling, the words and sparks fly between them. Each has secret, highly emo-
(continued)

tional reasons for being so involved in the subject they are investigating. As those secrets are gradually revealed, along with the plight of the children used in the racket, the intensity of Kelly's and Brant's growing love builds to a fever pitch. Another very special romance from Barbara Boswell!

That delightful duo Adrienne Staff and Sally Goldenbaum bring you a richly emotional, joyous romance in **KEVIN'S STORY,** LOVESWEPT #165. I'm sure many of you remember Kevin Ross who was befriended by Susan Rosten in **WHAT'S A NICE GIRL. . . ?** Kevin is now a successful businessman, seeking a model to be the spokeswoman for his product when gorgeous Suzy Keller sweeps into his life. It's love at first sight, but a love Kevin is determined to sabotage. Suzy isn't about to let that happen though . . . and she sets out to prove it in the most provocative ways possible. He may not be able to hear her passionate whispers, but he'll feel the force of her love every day, in every way!

In **LISTEN FOR THE DRUMMER,** LOVESWEPT #166, Joan Elliott Pickart will keep you chuckling while cheering on the romance of zany Brenna MacPhee and conservative Hunter Emerson. Brenna runs a pet hotel; Hunter runs a business. Brenna lives in a wildly unpredictable world; Hunter has everything in his life organized to a "T," including his wardrobe, composed exclusively of white shirts and dark suits and ties. Despite their differences he's unreasonably mad about the woman . . . especially when he discovers a need in her life as great as the one in his! Be sure not to miss this latest delight from Joan!

I've described **THE SHAMROCK TRINITY** before, but let me whet your appetite a bit more by
(continued)

reminding you that these three interrelated love stories are by Kay Hooper, Iris Johansen, and Fayrene Preston. On the back covers of the books we describe the Delaney brothers as "powerful men . . . rakes and charmers . . . they needed only love to make their lives complete." You'll learn how true those words are to your great pleasure when reading these never-to-be forgotten romances—**RAFE, THE MAVERICK** by Kay Hooper; **YORK, THE RENEGADE** by Iris Johansen; **BURKE, THE KINGPIN** by Fayrene Preston. Be sure to have your bookseller save copies of **THE SHAMROCK TRINITY** for you! We believe that **THE SHAMROCK TRINITY** continues the LOVESWEPT tradition of originality and freshness without sacrificing the beloved romance elements. We hope you'll agree and we will eagerly look forward to your response to this "first" in romance publishing. Enjoy the "Super Seven."

Warm regards,
Sincerely,

Carolyn Nichols

Carolyn Nichols
  Editor
LOVESWEPT
Bantam Books, Inc.
666 Fifth Avenue
New York, NY 10103